PHANTOM ENCOUNTER

When she reached the top of the stairs, the entire house was suddenly plunged into darkness. With a stifled scream Lauren felt for the flashlight she had left on a small table at the head of the stairs, but she couldn't find it in the dark. Her hands outscretched, she groped for her door and the light switch within.

Soft fingers closed over her wrist as she touched the switch and gently drew her hand away. Panic seized her, and she was unable to breathe, let alone scream.

All at once all the lights simultaneously came back on. A quick look around verified she was alone in the room.

Although her heart was still pounding, she found she wasn't quite as frightened as much as she was startled. It was as if — whatever — had sensed her fear and turned the lights back on to reassure her....

D1190071

Abigail
McDaniels

HOUSE OF FOUR SEASONS

LEISURE BOOKS   NEW YORK CITY

A LEISURE BOOK®

March 1992

Published by

Dorchester Publishing Co., Inc.
276 Fifth Avenue
New York, NY 10001

Printed in the United States of America.

HOUSE OF FOUR SEASONS

Chapter One

The old house sat a bit off-center on the lot, it's rippled glass panes catching the glint of sunlight and swallowing it up. Lauren loved it at first sight.

"It's exactly what I'm looking for," she said to the realtor, making no attempt to conceal her enthusiasm.

Surprisingly, Miss Jensen looked less than convinced. "It's been on the market for a while. The owner, a Mr. Nathaniel Padgett, died recently, and there being no heirs, the estate was put up for sale."

"It's lovely. Queen Anne, isn't it?" Lauren knew it was, but she wanted to discuss the merits of this wonderful old house with the woman, to admire it aloud. She could scarcely control her urge to run up the walk and onto the deep veranda.

"That's right. When I did the walk-through with the other realtors, I noticed there were still pieces of the original furnishings inside."

"What about his personal belongings?" A doubt clouded her eyes. "I mean, surely his things aren't—"

"No, no," Miss Jensen said with a short laugh. "As I've said, Mr. Padgett had no family. The executor of the estate removed all the personal belongings and as much of the furniture as was needed to pay off Mr. Padgett's debts. The remaining pieces are to be sold with the property. I suppose he thought that would be an inducement to a perspective buyer."

Lauren walked slowly up the walk which was cracked in places and bordered by a struggling bed of sweet william that was fighting for survival against the encroaching lawn. The grounds looked as if they had been left unattended for a long time. The bay window, a prominent feature of the ground floor, was flanked by spindly gardenias that amazingly sported a few velvety white blooms despite the obvious lack of pruning. A tangle of daisies bordered the veranda, and to either side of the house were jungles of oleander and more gardenias. The tall oaks out front were encircled with elephant ears that had proliferated through the years and now threatened to engulf the lawn, and huge magnolias sprawled in the side yard.

"The landscaping must have been magnificent at one time."

Miss Jensen nodded. "Now it's gone more or less to seed. Everything needs to be cut back and trimmed. There's a wisteria in the back whose trunk is as big around as your waist. if it were me, I'd cut it down before it damages the roof."

Lauren didn't answer. She loved wisteria. They went up the wooden steps and onto the porch. When a board creaked beneath the realtor's feet, Lauren looked at her questioningly.

"It's quite sound, I assure you, Miss Hamilton. Old houses just make noises." Miss Jensen looked around the porch and up at the vee-grooved ceiling. "Just as I thought. This ceiling was painted robin's egg blue. They usually were, you know."

Lauren nodded. She reached out and touched the nearest wall where the paint was cracked and peeling. "It needs work."

"I'm afraid the owner let it go during his last years. Structurally it's sound, but it needs a lot of TLC. Tender Loving Care," she added as if Lauren might not be familiar with the term. "That's why I didn't show it to you right away. This house really needs a man's touch."

"I'll have a husband soon," Lauren said with a quick smile. "I'm engaged. This house will be perfect for us."

"Perhaps you should have brought him with you. The amount of work it needs may seem overwhelming to him."

"Not Robert. You see, he will probably want to hire out the work. He isn't much use with a hammer or paintbrush. As a matter of fact, I'll do most of the cosmetic work myself. Decorating is one of my hobbies."

The realtor put her key in the lock-box and opened the front door.

Lauren stepped in and felt a breeze rush past her and through the house as if it had sighed. She hesitated before going in farther.

"All the paneling here is original. So is the wallpaper—unfortunately. Tastes have changed quite a bit in eighty years."

"Eighty years? That's how old it is?"

"More or less. Queen Anne houses were already going out of fashion by the turn of the century so I don't know why the man built one."

"I suppose he liked the style." Lauren found herself disliking the woman's outspoken opinions and wondered if she was truly interested in selling the house. "Maybe he was a romantic."

"The living room is in here."

"Parlor."

"I beg your pardon?"

"It would have been called a parlor."

Miss Jensen heaved an exasperated sigh. "Whatever. As you can see it has beautiful detailing in the fireplace. Look at those cornice moldings."

Lauren needed no instructions; she had already seen the beautifully detailed work. She lightly ran her fingers over the ornately carved mantelpiece. "No dust," she mused.

"I suppose they made houses tighter then. Or maybe someone leaned against the mantel when they moved out the living room furniture." She touched one of the heavy damask curtains. "There's plenty of dust in these."

The wallpaper here was dark maroon with a gold pattern that was both opulent and oppressive, an obvious holdover of the owner's Victorian taste. Through the years, the deep colors had faded as was evidenced by darker squares of the wallpaper about the room where large pictures had hung. Lauren wondered if the adornment of the walls had been with oil paintings or merely cheap prints. "Why did he die?" she heard herself asking.

"The owner? It was of natural causes. He was a hundred years old."

"He was? I never knew anyone who lived to be that old."

Miss Jensen let out another short burst of laughter. "He was known as the town eccentric, because of his extreme age, no doubt. He was an old man for as long as most of us can remember."

Lauren wondered what she had meant by eccentric but decided not to ask. For a person like Miss Jensen that definition might apply to a whole range of behavior from a person who didn't mow his yard regularly to one who kept cats.

"The dining room is through here. One of

the interesting features of this house are the pocket doors that divide several of the larger rooms. At the office we've speculated this was done to provide party space and room for dancing." She gave Lauren a wink. "Old Mr. Padgett may have 'cut a rug' as they used to say. At any rate, the house is perfectly designed for parties."

"Did he have people in often?"

"Not to my knowledge. You have to realize, however, that he must have been in his late sixties when we were born," Miss Jensen said. Lauren gave her a cool look. "Perhaps he had dances when he was younger."

Lauren tried not to mind that the woman had inadvertently hit upon an issue of great sensitivity to her. She was already in her mid-thirties and had been more or less engaged to Robert Kinney for seven years. At times she wondered if they would ever get around to being married. She had already resigned herself to the fact that at her age she would probably not have children, a situation that didn't distress her nearly as much as it did her family and friends.

Miss Jensen led her back into the wide hall beside the staircase. "Storage under there," she said as if it were an afterthought.

"I suppose that would be the formal parlor and library behind this wall?"

"Why, yes. How did you know?"

Lauren had surprised even herself with the accuracy of her guess, although it wasn't altogether uneducated. "The old houses of this style were often arranged that way. The 'masculine' rooms to the right and the 'feminine' ones to the left. Only," she looked aware for the first time that this house didn't hold to convention, "it's just the opposite here, isn't it?"

"If you say so. I don't know much about old houses. I prefer nice, clean tract homes." A blush colored her cheeks as she realized her faux pas and quickly added, "These old beauties certainly have their charm though."

Moving hastily, Miss Jensen pushed open the double oak doors and led Lauren through the formal parlor and into the oak paneled library. Lauren's mouth dropped open. "The books are still here—and there are so many of them."

"You can throw them out if you like. I'm sure none of them are valuable."

Lauren frowned at the woman. Had she been so disagreeable all day? Lauren hadn't noticed. "I'll do no such thing. I love books."

The room was large with double windows and padded window seats. One corner rounded out into the base of the turret Lauren had noticed from the outside. On sunny days the room would be a perfect place to read or sketch her preliminary house plans. The architectural firm let her do some of her work at home. The rest of the room was filled from top to bottom with oak shelves stuffed with row upon row of books. Another fireplace, this one of black marble, dominated one wall. Several logs, dusty now, had been arranged on the grate as if someone had meant to use the fireplace but had not done so.

In the center of the room was an enormous desk. Lauren went to it and pulled open one of the drawers.

"It's all empty," Miss Jensen said. "I guess it's still here because no one could get it through the doors."

Lauren looked around. "How did it get in here?"

"Who knows? Maybe a wall was added after it was in place. Or maybe it took root and grew there. The floor is dirty enough."

Usually Lauren prided herself on having a sense of humor, but she saw nothing funny about the realtor's remarks. This house had a nostalgic sadness as if everyone who had loved it had died. She found herself wondering if houses ever got lonely. Lauren had always had a fanciful side to her. It was one of the things Robert liked least.

Through the doorway in the back wall, she glanced into the drawing room. The colors there were as heavy and oppressive as all the rest of the house, but she thought with some work it might make a perfect office for her drafting board and filing cabinets. A door on the opposite side was open to the central hall, across which was the dining room.

The kitchen, in the back of the house, jutted out at an angle enclosing the old well. The appliances were outdated, but there was a surplus of cabinets and counter space.

"I know this seems odd," Lauren said, "but I'm disoriented. Which way is the front of the house?"

"It's that way," the realtor indicated vaguely, seeming a bit uncertain herself. "I had that same problem when I came here the first time or two. I suppose it's the series of pantries we came through between the dining and drawing rooms. The whole house has curious angles. I suspect Mr. Padgett was his own architect."

"That could explain it, I suppose." As an architect herself, Lauren was reluctant to admit to losing her sense of direction in a house. "Any hidden passages?" she asked, half-teasing.

"None that I'm aware of." Miss Jensen's expression was solemn. "Some of the rooms don't seem to meet exactly, but that could be due to the odd angles where this wing and the turret meet the house."

Lauren ignored the woman's humorless reply and retraced her steps back through the maze of pantries and into the central hall. By craning her neck she could see up the center of the stairwell to the attic level of the house. "Three stories?"

"Two actually. The attic isn't finished out into rooms."

"But from outside I thought..." Lauren shook her head. This wasn't the time or place to let her imagination run wild. Miss Jensen would think her a fool.

15

As they climbed the stairs, the treads creaked in their wake. Lauren looked back but saw nothing, and as Miss Jensen seemed determined to ignore it, Lauren decided she would, too, though it did seem curious. Along the wall next to the stairs were more brightly colored patches of wallpaper, reminders of paintings or perhaps family portraits which had been removed. On the first landing stood a silent grandfather clock.

"I can't believe this beautiful old clock would go with the house," Lauren said. "It's much too valuable."

"Not really. None of us could get it to work. The key doesn't seem to fit."

"Perhaps it could be repaired." Lauren was beginning to wonder if Miss Jensen was operating in the estate executor's best interest.

"If you don't want it I'm sure we could take it away. I assume it was left as a selling point."

Lauren looked at it suspiciously. "I just wouldn't want to be accused of keeping something that isn't mine." She touched the cherry wood frame and noticed that it, like the mantel below, wasn't at all dusty. For a moment she was puzzled, then she remembered Miss Jensen had said someone had tried to start it. Naturally it wouldn't be dusty if it had been handled recently.

They continued up to the second floor. Instead of the narrow hallway Lauren had expected there, she found herself in a large, windowless area which apparently served as a foyer to the four bedrooms which opened off it like the four points of a compass.

The rooms were all spacious and of approximately equal size. The two on either side shared bathrooms which had evidently been added after the original construction of the house. None of the bedrooms was square, but instead each was L-shaped, wrapping around the center foyer, and the one with dark yellow paper jutted out over the angle in the kitchen below where the well stood.

"Very sunny," Miss Jensen said. "Good views," she hurriedly added.

The realtor seemed ill-at-ease. "Yes, there is a lovely view." The room they were in was predominantly blue, and through the windows in the turret corner she could see the small lake out back which was shared by the neighboring residents. Beyond the lake was a swampy marsh with gray skeins of Spanish moss dripping from the limbs of huge live oaks.

"What are the neighbors like?"

"Most of them are about our age with young teenage children. In a few years all their kids will graduate from school and move away, and the place will be even quieter. Actually, I doubt you can hear any children now, since this house sits farther down the road than the others."

There was that reference to age again. Lauren wondered if the woman was being deliberately irritating. But for what reason?

She circled the second floor again, going from

17

one unique room to the next by way of the interconnecting doors. Each of the different color schemes was reinforced by a wide border of colored glass of the same hue around the windows.

"You can see now why the house is called Four Seasons," Miss Jensen pointed out. "This is the Autumn room so it has yellow panes and yellow walls. Summer is red, spring green, winter blue. See?"

"Yes, I see." Personally she thought the idea was rather contrived, but it would offer interesting decorating possibilities. "I'll put you in the Summer Suite," she could say, or "I'm certain you'd be more comfortable in the Autumn Room." She shook her head, redirecting her attention to Miss Jensen.

"You could move in immediately," she was saying.

"What? Yes, yes, I suppose I could." She stopped in the Winter room for a closer inspection of its oversized bed with its imposing mahogany inlaid headboard and side rails that curved into the rolled footboard. "It's easy to see why this was left behind."

"Lovely, isn't it?" Miss Jensen seemed to have to force cheerfulness into her voice. "It's called a sleigh bed. Museum quality, really. It has a queen-sized mattress—I measured."

"Most antique beds aren't this large." Lauren ran her hand over the curved footboard. "It really does look like an old-fashioned sleigh. To be pulled by nightmares?" she quipped, trying to get Miss Jensen to smile, but the woman had already turned away.

The steps to the attic were steeper and narrower than the others had been. At the top was the dark, narrow hall she had expected on the bedroom level. "This is an attic?"

"I'm not sure why it was arranged like this. Perhaps Mr. Padgett planned to eventually divide the sides up into servants' rooms." She opened the nearest door. "This is the only one that serves as a bedroom."

The dark room had a sloped ceiling, apparently following the steep roof line. There was space enough for a narrow bed and a small dresser but nothing else.

"It looks more like a cell than a bedroom," Lauren observed.

"Servants' working conditions have improved so much over this century." By the tone of Miss Jensen's voice, Lauren wasn't sure that the woman was entirely in favor of the change.

"Poe or Dickens would have loved this place," Lauren said as she led the inspection of the long, barracks-like rooms on either side of the hall, empty of all but a few forgotten piles of papers and cast-off items. As they stepped around and over the litter, their footsteps echoed on the grimy floorboards. Apparently to Miss Jensen's satisfaction, Lauren was soon convinced she'd seen all she wanted of the attic.

As they passed the servant's room again Lauren paused. "How sad the maid must have been up here all alone with this dismal attic all around her."

"She probably never thought twice about it. At least she had her privacy. That's more than can be said for the second-floor bedrooms," the realtor went on to say as they went back downstairs. "Why anyone would want interconnecting doors between all the bedrooms, I'll never understand."

"It's not uncommon in houses of this vintage," Lauren explained. "Perhaps one was for the husband, another for his wife, the other two for their children. The privacy needs of people today are different than they were many years ago."

"Of course, this wouldn't be a problem," Miss Jensen rushed to explain, realizing her blunder. "If it were me, I'd simply arrange furniture in front of them. Just because they are there doesn't mean they have to be used."

"That's true." She went back into the blue room and gazed out at the lake.

"So what do you think?" Miss Jensen said with a covert glace at her watch. "Are you interested in this house?"

"It's awfully big. It needs a lot of work." Lauren heard a soft creak that sounded as if someone standing on the wood floor in the room directly below them had shifted his weight from one foot to another. But that was impossible, as she was sure no one else was in the house with them. She wondered how long it would take her to become accustomed to the noises. "I don't even know if it's in my price range. And it's right on the swamp."

Miss Jensen beamed. "I was saving the good news for last." She named a figure that made Lauren's eyes widen.

"Surely you're mistaken. This house must be worth far more than that."

"No, it's the age, you see. It needs some re-wiring and has no central heating or air-conditioning. You know how hot Louisiana gets in the summer."

"Yes, but . . ."

"And it needs paint and wallpaper through-out. The plumbing is good, though. It's all fairly new. The roof is sound, and this house could ride out a hurricane—not that they come this far inland without losing most of their force. As for the swamp, why, that's Siddel Marsh. The town is named for it. It's a local landmark."

"We aren't that far south of Shreveport. I'd think a commuter family would snap this up fast."

"You must be new around here. Folks in these parts aren't that fond of commuting, not like they do in big cities."

Lauren refrained from pointing out that Shreveport *was* a big city. "I've lived here eight years. I work for Newton and Combe."

Miss Jensen nodded. "You're still a new-comer. Siddel Marsh residents usually work and live here in town. Being on the edge of town as it is, Four Seasons seems inconvenient for most people."

Lauren hid her smile. She still hadn't grown accustomed to the small town ways of life. If she hadn't been offered such a good job with the architectural firm, she would never have considered moving to Siddel Marsh, but the job wasn't the only thing that had kept her here. She had met Robert Kinney her first day on the job. Within a few weeks they had started seeing each other, and the dating had steadily continued ever since. Robert was a native, born and bred, and couldn't imagine living anywhere else. Lauren supposed she would live in this town forever and eventually lose the stigma of newcomer.

"Of course at this price it won't be on the market long," Miss Jensen added. "One of the realtors at Appleway showed it this morning."

Lauren smiled. She had yet to see any property that wasn't being presumably considered by some nebulous client. At least Miss Jensen wasn't so obvious as to imply a contract could already be written on it. "I'll take it."

"You will?" The realtor looked frankly amazed, then caught herself. "You'll be so happy here. You've made a wise decision."

"I'll give my landlady notice immediately. That way I'll be able to move in as soon as the paperwork is done." As Lauren took a final look around, she noticed the wallpaper was sagging even worse than she had realized. "I can see how I'll spend my vacation time this year," she said, but she wasn't disheartened. She knew she was getting a real bargain, and the physical activity would be good for her.

The paperwork on the house went through surprisingly fast, almost as though the realtor was afraid Lauren would change her mind. Because of her job and excellent credit rating, Lauren found it easy to secure a mortgage. She was a bit surprised to find everything falling into place so neatly, almost as if she were indeed meant to have the house. The day she moved in was prophetically sunny.

The movers had deposited most of her belongings in a heap in the dining room, but she had convinced them into moving the heavy bedroom furniture upstairs into the Autumn room with its mustard yellow hues. She would have preferred to occupy the Winter room, but first she had to figure a way to remove the huge bed that was already there. Lauren appreciated its antique beauty, but she couldn't imagine wanting to actually sleep in it.

Lauren decided to unpack the kitchen and bedroom first so she would be able to eat and sleep in comfort. On her way upstairs to get started, she paused on the landing and looked down at the oak floor of the central hallway and up at the medallioned ceiling that supported the hall chandelier. Pride of ownership flooded through her. She had never before owned her own home, and she was exhilarated by being mistress over all that surrounded her. As she lovingly caressed the mahogany bannister, a feeling of peace settled around her.

The movers had placed her bed in the Autumn room in such a way that, when lying on it, to her left she could see into the bathroom and through the interconnecting doorway to the blue room; to her right she could see into the red room. Straight ahead were the windows which afforded her a picturesque though not spectacular view of a part of the lake and swamp.

She soon had the room in presentable order, though it would have to be turned upside down when she started on the walls. Lauren looked at the dismal wallpaper and wondered why anyone had ever chosen such a dreary design and color combination for a bedroom.

Another look at the blue room confirmed her earlier decision to take that room for her own as soon as possible. Although the heavy colors of navy and maroon were overwhelming to her, anything was better than that sickly yellow.

After unpacking her dishes and silverware and the other items she would need to cook and clean, Lauren changed from her grimy jeans and sweat shirt to a clean outfit and headed for the local paint store.

An hour later, the trunk of her car was filled to overflowing with materials and her monthly budget was severely strained, but she was sure she had enough supplies to tackle most of the house's interior redecorating needs.

She parked behind her house in a garage which had at one time been a carriage house. The fading light from the setting sun gave a surreal color to the flowers and the numerous clumps of wisteria. Lauren tilted her head to one side as she considered the giant vine. From that angle, it seemed bent on consuming the back half of the house.

Her eyes followed the twisting limbs upward to the turret room. She stiffened. Someone seemed to be standing there in the window, gazing down at her. A moment later, the clouds shifted, and she recognized the reflection of a tree on the glass. Feeling foolish Lauren took her paint and paper into the house.

For the rest of the evening she worked on the kitchen. Years of grime would have to be scrubbed from the woodwork, and the wall and floor coverings would have to be replaced.

Gingerly, she stripped the flaking paper off the walls and stuffed it into garbage bags. Removing the rust-red linoleum, which was worn down to the backing in spots, proved to be impossible. She would have to cover it with new sheet vinyl and hope it would adhere.

A noise from upstairs startled Lauren, and she looked up sharply. It had been soft and of short duration, ill-defined and unfamiliar. Had it been a branch scraping the side of the house? Rats in the attic?

Moving as silently as possible, Lauren went to the foot of the stairs and looked up into the blackness. She strained to listen, but heard nothing. As she flipped on the switch to light the stairway, she heard the sound again, but it was gone as quickly as before.

Swallowing the lump in her throat, Lauren began climbing the stairs. Her sneakers were silent on the wooden treads, but almost at once she heard the steps creak behind her as if someone were following her a few paces back. A sharp glance over her shoulder proved she was alone, but a shiver ran up her spine.

"This won't do," she told herself firmly. She was an intelligent adult, and she wasn't going to creep about her own house as if she were a frightened child. She was positive she was alone in the house. There had to be some logical, plausible cause for the noise other than an intruder, and once she found it, she knew she would feel silly for being frightened.

With determination she went up the stairs, not bothering to move quietly, and as soon as she reached the top of the stairs, she turned on the lights in the upper foyer that surrounded the stairwell. Everything looked as it had before.

One by one she checked the rooms, ending with her yellow bedroom. Nothing was out of place. She stepped back out into the foyer and looked up the stairwell to the attic. She didn't feel up to groping her way through the cavernous rooms above, so she assured herself that she had imagined the noises and gave up the search.

Feeling a bit sore from the unaccustomed

work, Lauren decided to call it a day and went back to her bedroom, carefully closing her door behind her. She knew it was late but was surprised to find it was well after midnight. Time had passed so quickly.

She shucked off her clothes and tossed them in the laundry hamper before turning on the tub. She felt sticky from all her work and was looking forward to soaking clean. As she turned off the water the pipes knocked, and she jumped in fright.

With a foolish grin she got into the tub. The noise she heard earlier could have been pipes banging in the attic or any of a dozen other things. As she soaked, her sore muscles began to relax, and although the bath was soothing, she decided that she would have to add a shower head, for she truly preferred showers to baths.

When she was finished bathing, Lauren put on her terry cloth bathrobe and padded barefoot onto the worn Turkish rug that covered her bedroom floor. Each of the bedrooms had similar floor coverings, coordinated with the room's color scheme. Her first thought had been to replace them as they were quite frayed, but she liked their antique charm and decided to try a professional carpet cleaner first.

Humming softly she searched for her hairbrush. She knew it was unpacked because she had used it before going to the store. Now she couldn't find it anywhere.

She stopped humming and went back into

the bathroom she shared with the Winter room. The brush wasn't on the marble countertop or behind the beveled-glass mirrored door of her medicine cabinet. As she looked about, she noticed the door that led to the blue room was open a crack. Had she gone in there as she was brushing her hair? She pushed open the door and took a step into the shadowy room.

The silvery moonlight was kind to the room, harmonizing with the blues of the wallpaper and rug. For a time, she stared into the dimly lit interior, delighting in its magic, then she flipped on the light switch, flooding the room with brilliance so she could resume her search. Because of the way the room wrapped about the foyer, she couldn't see the sleigh bed from where she stood.

Suddenly Lauren felt cool as if a breeze had touched her. After a pause she went around the corner. The room was as empty as the others had been. Lauren went to the window and looked out at the lake. A mist was rising, and tendrils curled about the trunks of the trees nearest the water. The gray moss swirled in a silent dance as if it were reaching for the fog. For a moment she thought she saw someone standing in the shadows of the trees nearest the house, but she told herself this visage was no more real than the shadow on the window earlier. She went to the other side of the turret windows and looked down at the garage. She could clearly see where she had stood earlier.

Lauren backed away from the window and turned to go back to her room.

There in the center of the big sleigh bed was her hairbrush.

How had it gotten there? she wondered. As she stretched across the bed to reach her brush, it suddenly dawned on her that she wouldn't have put it down in such an inconvenient place. When her fingers closed around the handle, she snatched it to her. Suddenly the room seemed too big and empty.

Telling herself she was being foolish, Lauren hastily retreated to her own room.

Chapter Two

Lauren walked through her house, feeling a keen sense of satisfaction. After weeks of work the wood gleamed with golden depths, new and cheerful paper covered the downstairs rooms, and the oak floor had been buffed to a reflecting glow. She had used every day of her vacation to do it, but the old house had come alive for her, and tonight all her friends would see it as well.

She supposed it had been whimsical of her not to have shown it to anyone sooner—not Robert, not even her best friend, Celia Malone—but she knew they would have been discouraging about the project. The amount of required work would have daunted most anyone. Lauren, however, liked work or rather detested idleness. In her years at Newton and Combe she had only taken vacation days whenever her employers had insisted that she should.

The spring nights were still cool so Lauren lit candles and oil lamps throughout the downstairs. The delicate aroma of warm, scented wax mixed with the heady fragrance of wisteria that floated in through the open windows, and the furniture smelled faintly of lemon oil. Beneath it all was a trace of spicy scent that vaguely reminded Lauren of a cologne her grandfather had worn. As she was puzzling over which of the oils or cleaning agents she'd used might have left behind this scent, her first guest arrived.

"Celia! Come in. Tell me what you think." Lauren ushered her friend in and waited expectantly.

"It's beautiful." Celia moved farther into the hall beyond the entry foyer and looked about in wonder. "How on earth did you find such a dream?"

"Just luck, I guess. Actually it looked nothing like this when I first saw it. The wallpaper was so dark and hideous it would have turned your stomach." The house settled audibly. "Don't pay the noises any attention. I paid extra for them."

They laughed companionably and went into the front parlor. Lauren had covered the dark walls with a white paper with pastel blue stripes separating pale pink roses, and she had replaced the rotten damask curtains with white lace that added to the room's brightness.

"Elegant! You should forget architecture and go into interior design."

"I only know what I like."

Celia looked around the room. "I've lived in this town for years and never even noticed this place. I must have driven by it dozens of times."

"It has fallen into disrepair. Fortunately it's too dark outside for you to have noticed I haven't had time to tackle the outside yet. I'm hoping Robert will volunteer to help. I'm not fond of ladders."

"I love the way it smells. What is that? Clove?"

"I suppose it's from one of the cleaners I used. I've scrubbed in here with everything on the market. Maybe you smell the wisteria."

"Wisteria? I thought the wisteria stopped blooming weeks ago." Celia sniffed again. "I never smelled a cleaner like that. I'm sure it's the scent of cloves."

"Come look at the rest of the house before anyone else arrives."

With enthusiasm, Celia followed Lauren's quick steps upstairs, but as they neared the second-floor landing, Celia's steps slowed and faltered. "What's wrong?" Lauren asked.

Celia paused, then smiled. "Nothing. Nothing at all," she said, then hurried up the remaining steps.

"I'm going to put rattan furniture here in

the foyer," Lauren was saying. "It's a dark spot since there are no windows, and heavy furniture would overpower it. Don't you think so?"

Celia nodded from the top of the stairs where she had stopped. She was looking up at the narrow flight of stairs ahead of her. "What's up there?"

"Nothing really. Just attic space and a servant's room. It's the most dismal place you can imagine. I doubt I'll ever use it for anything. Come see the bedrooms."

Lauren opened the door to the red room and entered, gesturing with a flourish of her hand for Celia to follow. Celia, however, lingered near the door.

"It's hard to tell now," Lauren said, "but when it's light outside and you look through the colored glass surrounding the window, it suggests a season. This is summer. Each room is a different season and that's how the house got its name."

Celia silently followed Lauren into the green room, then the yellow one. "You sleep in here?" Celia asked, breaking the silence.

"Aren't these yellows awful? I'll repaper this room next."

"Aren't you afraid this wallpaper might flutter down on you during the night? I would be."

"It's cozy up here," Lauren protested with a slight edge to her voice. "You should see the view—especially from in here." She pushed open the door to the blue room and confidently stepped in.

Celia hesitated at the doorway. "The colors are so dark. How could anyone do this to a bedroom?"

"Tastes have changed over the past eighty years. This house must have been the epitome of style at the turn of the century. After looking at the colors for the past weeks I've rather grown to like them myself." She ignored Celia's astonished look. "Come around the corner and look at this."

Reluctantly, Celia stepped farther into the room and beheld the sleigh bed. "Someone slept in that?"

"Sure did. As this was the master bedroom, my guess is that the owner slept here every night for at least eighty years. I'm not sure exactly when the house was completed."

"The same man lived here all that time?"

Lauren nodded. "The realtor said he was a hundred years old when he died."

Celia looked back at the bed. "Did he die in here? This bed looks like a killer to me."

Lauren frowned. "That's not funny, Celia. I have no idea where he died, but I assume it was in a hospital or maybe a rest home."

"I'm sorry. That was in poor taste, wasn't it? I only meant the bed is so ... gothic."

"It's probably priceless." Lauren still felt defensive. "The only reason it was left behind was because it couldn't be removed. The doorways are too narrow, and it would never make it around the bend in the stairs. I rather like it. I may take this room for my own."

"Now I *know* you're kidding." Celia went to the corner that rounded out into the turret. "You have a lovely view of the lake. Look at that moonlight shining on it."

Somewhat mollified that her friend had finally said something complimentary, Lauren came to her. "That's what I like about this room. You know how I love water. And this room is larger than the others, thanks to the turret. If I put chairs here, it will be a lovely place to read or sketch."

"Can't you see the neighbors' houses?"

"Not from here. You're turned around—the house does that until you get used to it. We're directly over the library. The neighbors are off the green room. No one lives back here because of the swamp. The next house on this side is a farmhouse a quarter mile down the road. I sit at the very edge of town."

"Don't you get lonely out here?"

"Are you kidding? I haven't had time to turn around, much less feel lonely. That's why I haven't had you out before now. Plus, I wanted to get some things done first so the house would make a good impression on you."

"If the downstairs looked anything like this floor does when you started, you've worked miracles." Celia leaned forward. "Who is that down there? See? In those trees?"

Lauren looked past her to the dark clump of saplings in the yard below. "Your eyes are playing tricks on you. It's just shadows and Spanish moss moving about in the wind."

Celia turned and was staring at the bed and the long imprint in its coverlet. "But I'm sure I saw—"

"Listen! There's the doorbell. I'll bet you just saw one of the other guests out there," Lauren suggested as she rushed out of the room.

"Lauren, have you actually been lying on this thing?" she asked before realizing she was alone. Hastily, she hurried after her hostess.

As the guests arrived, some alone, others in couples or small groups, the downstairs filled with conversation and laughter. The last of the guests to arrive was Robert Kinney.

"Finally!" Lauren said as she ushered him in. "I was beginning to think you weren't going to come."

"I wanted to call and say I would be late. I thought you said the phone was supposed to be installed yesterday."

"They've put me off again until some time next week. Now they have decided I'm too far away from the neighbors to tie into their line, and they have to set some poles and run more wire or something."

Robert took a step in and uneasily looked around. "When you sent me the invitation I couldn't believe this was the right address. You bought the old Padgett house."

"Yes, I know. Did you know him?"

"No way. All of us kids were scared to death of him. He didn't want us anywhere near the place."

"I can see why an old bachelor wouldn't

want to be bothered by a bunch of kids. The realtor said he was eccentric."

"That's one way to put it. Everybody in town called him crazy."

A cold breeze passed through the house, stirring the candle flames.

"Come in and close the door, Robert. The night is turning cool."

She ushered him into the dining room where most of the guests were gathered about the hors d'oeuvres. "Make yourself at home, Robert," she said over the din. "Wine and soft drinks are on the sideboard. I need to see if any of the others want anything."

Lauren edged through the crowd and eventually made her way into the living room. For some reason she felt resentful that Robert hadn't seen how beautiful the house was. She wanted to hear what a lovely job she had done, not about how crazy its former owner had been. She was still unreasonably miffed at Celia's reaction to the bedrooms, too. They needed work, but Lauren didn't think they were all that bad.

"Lauren?"

She turned to see Susan Redlow, a secretary who worked for the same firm as Lauren and Robert. "Hello, Susan. I didn't see you come in."

Susan responded with her mousy smile and shoved her glasses up the bridge of her nose. "I slipped in with some others. I brought you this."

"You weren't supposed to bring gifts," Lauren protested with a smile. "This is just a party, not a housewarming."

"I know, but when I saw this I knew it had to belong to you." She handed Lauren a wrapped package.

Lauren wasn't sure what to do with it. To open it there might make her other guests feel they should have brought something, but to set it aside to be opened later might hurt Susan's feelings. "Come with me. I'll find us a quieter place for this."

They crossed the back hall to the unoccupied drawing room. By the time Lauren had started working on this room, she had fallen under the house's charm, and consequently the wallpaper she had selected was medium green with a chintz-like floral design. The windows looked out onto the back porch and the twisted trunk of the wisteria that was as large around as a tree. Lauren glanced at the area of the yard where Celia earlier had thought she had seen someone standing, but she couldn't see the smaller trees at all in the darkness beyond the lighted porch.

"I like your house," Susan said as if she were a child repeating what she had been schooled to say. "It's so big."

"Thank you. I like it even more than I thought I would, to tell you the truth. At first I was afraid I would rattle around in here all alone."

Susan nodded as if she understood. "I'm not

sure I'd be comfortable alone in such a big house."

"Well, I'm not entirely alone," Lauren felt compelled to point out. "The Barkers live right next door."

"I know but they're so seldom home. Since Fred Barker retired, they travel between their kids' houses in Utah and Florida almost constantly, not to mention vacations. They practically live in their Winnebago."

"I didn't realize that." Lauren sat on the bottle green sofa and began unwrapping the gift. She hoped it wasn't a print. She was particular about the pictures she wanted to hang on these walls, and the package was about the right size for one. Worse, it might be one of Susan's watercolors. Lauren forced herself to smile at her guest.

The heavy paper fell away, revealing a walnut board with the alphabet and numbers inlaid in mother-of-pearl. For a moment, she stared at the gift, at a loss for words. "It's lovely," she finally said.

"It's a Ouija board."

"Yes. Yes, I know what it is. But Susan, I don't believe in—"

"It was so pretty, and I know how you like antiques. I couldn't resist it—literally. Somehow it seemed to cry out to me." She gave Lauren a weak smile that she must have meant to be apologetic and added, "Not really, of course, but you know what I mean."

Lauren tilted the board to catch the lamplight. "It's beautiful. I've never seen one quite like it." The deep brown wood had been burnished to a sheen, and the contrasting light letters and numbers had the translucence of the shells from which they had been fashioned. The other inlaid designs in the wood had been fashioned from bits of a bright red wood that wasn't familiar to Lauren. The mahogany planchette differed from any others she had seen in that it was in the shape of a triangle and had a natural crystal as a pointer. "It must have been terribly expensive, Susan. You really shouldn't have."

"It wasn't, really. I was the only one in the store, and I think the antique dealer was glad to have any customer at all. He made me a good price."

"How old do you suppose it is?" Lauren ran her fingers over the glossy wood and was surprised to feel her fingertips tingle.

"He didn't know anything about its history. He said it showed up as part of an estate sale several months ago."

Lauren looked up and smiled. "Thank you, Susan. I can't tell you how touched I am."

Susan blushed as she shyly smiled. "It's nice to have a friend to give gifts to."

Lauren liked the thoughtfulness behind the gift, but she wasn't too sure she wanted to foster Susan's friendship. Susan seemed to be the clinging type who would be under Lauren's feet every minute, if she were encouraged. Lauren set the Ouija board on a game table in a corner of the room where the soft glow from one of the lamps fell across it. "See how nice it looks here? It's the perfect place for it."

Susan looked doubtful but said nothing. As Lauren ushered her back to the other guests, she had an awkward feeling that Susan had intended for her to use the gift she had brought at the party. Lauren could just imagine what Robert would have to say about that.

She found Robert alone in the front parlor, stalking about the room as if he were making an inspection. "How do you like it?" she asked.

He turned to her with a frown but said, "You've done a good job on it."

"Why do I get the feeling that you're saying the opposite of what you mean?"

"You have done good work here. I mean that. It's just that I can't believe you bought this place at all."

She laughed as she moved closer to him. "Superstitious, Robert? I would never have guessed it."

He didn't dignify her teasing with an answer. "And there's so much to do in an old place like this. Are the foundations sound?"

"It's as sturdy as an oak tree. The roof doesn't even leak. All it needs is paint and a good scrubbing."

"It needs a lot more than that, and you know it."

"Yes, I do, but it was a marvelous buy. I got twice the house for my money and one with a history as well as character. I'm tired of sterile apartments with off-white walls and sensible carpets."

Robert snorted his disagreement.

Lauren took his arm and gazed up at him in her most entreating manner. "I was hoping you'd volunteer to help me with some of the exterior work."

His frown returned.

"After we're married this will be your home, too."

"What?"

"Well, you don't expect me to leave a house that's practically a mansion and move to a tract home with no trees and a larger monthly payment, do you? That's not reasonable."

"Lauren, if you planned for this to be our home, why wasn't I consulted?"

She glanced toward the hall that separated them from the other guests. "Please don't raise your voice, Robert. I didn't consult you because the idea never occurred to me until after I had bought the house and started working on it. It would be perfect for a family. Upstairs there are three extra bedrooms, plus a huge attic that could serve as a playroom for children on rainy days."

He looked unconvinced.

"I can't leave my guests to give you a tour now, but if you'll stay after they leave, I'll show you through." She drew him back across the hall to where the party was in full swing.

To Lauren's dismay, by ten o'clock most of her guests had gone. Susan Redlow, however, was still there, hanging back as if she were too shy to announce her departure and had been too shy to join in with the others as they left. Celia Malone and a man she often dated, Mark Edwards, remained as well, along with Robert.

"What a bunch of wet blankets," Celia complained. "The night is still young and almost everybody has already left."

"Maybe they all had to get up early tomorrow," Lauren said to cover her own disappointment.

"On Sunday?" Celia stacked up a pile of dishes to carry into the kitchen. "We may as well get these out of the way."

"Nonsense," Lauren said staunchly. "The party's not over until the last guest leaves."

"That's right," Mark seconded. "Let's play a game or something."

Susan spoke up for the first time in hours. "There's one in the drawing room. A game." She glanced sideways at Lauren.

Lauren opened her mouth to object, but Mark was already on his feet and pulling Celia toward the door. For a moment Lauren had a sensation of vertigo—of being swept away against her will. Then she saw the small smile on Susan's lips, and she got hold of herself. "I'd rather not just now," she said.

"Why not?" Celia said flippantly. "We can't let the party die on its feet, can we?"

Lauren didn't know what to say. She wasn't sure why she suddenly objected to them playing with the Ouija board. It was merely a

43

game. A cardboard version could be bought in any toy store. Silently, she followed her guests to the drawing room.

"Why, it's a Ouija board," Celia exclaimed when she reached the table. "I haven't played with one in years."

Robert's face stiffened as Lauren had expected. If he objected to her living in the old Padgett house, he was certain to be upset over her owning a Ouija board. "Susan gave it to me," she told him almost defensively.

Celia sat down opposite Mark. "Put your fingers on the planchette." He did as she said, and a silence grew around the table.

"Nothing is happening," he said at last.

"Concentrate." In a mysterious voice she said, "Is there anybody there?"

"Come on, Celia," Robert protested. "This is nonsense."

The planchette remained perfectly still. "Here, let me try," Susan said as Mark took his hand away. She sat in his chair and put her hand on the pointer facing Celia, then closed her eyes.

"Everybody concentrate," Celia whispered. "Is anybody there? Come talk to us."

Lauren found herself holding her breath. Slowly the planchette began to move. "W... E...L..." Mark repeated as the planchette moved slowly from one letter to another. "That doesn't spell anything."

Celia and Susan concentrated harder. More

quickly than before, the pointer selected the letters L A U R A.

"You made it do that," Robert said accusingly.

"I did not," Celia objected. "If I was moving it, I would have spelled Lauren's name correctly."

"This is all a bunch of bunk." Robert looked as if the whole business offended him.

"Lauren, you try it," Susan urged. "Take my place."

Lauren didn't want to, but she felt she had no choice. She didn't want to appear as ridiculous as Robert over a childish game. Reluctantly she sat down, and Celia put the board between them. "What do I do?"

"Don't tell me you've never played with a Ouija board," Celia said with a laugh. "Just rest your fingertips on the planchette and don't press down. That's right."

Almost at once Lauren felt a tingle begin in her fingers and race up her arms. Immediately the planchette began to swing in wide arcs that took it almost off the board.

"Hey, look at that!" Mark's voice was filled with awe.

"Lauren is doing it," Robert growled. "Quit kidding around."

Lauren's eyes were wide. "Celia, are you moving it?"

"No!"

Abruptly the crystal pointer swung to the W.

"Here we go again," Mark said.

The pointer spelled out "W E L C O M E" in such speedy jerks that Lauren had trouble keeping her fingers in contact with it. Then it spelled "L A U R A." As suddenly as it had started, the planchette stopped.

Lauren's eyes met Celia's. At last Celia said, "I guess we're talking to someone named Laura." At once the crystal flew to the word "NO."

"What is your name?" Susan ventured, her eyes nearly as wide as Lauren's.

"W E L C O M E   H O M E." Once more the planchette stopped.

Lauren took her hands away and put them under the table. "I don't like this."

"Don't be silly," Robert said in a testy voice. "This is just a toy. Move over and I'll prove it." He slid into Lauren's place as she vacated it. He put his hand on the planchette. It started to move even wilder than before. "O U T." It spelled the same word over and over with increasing speed until the planchette clattered loudly to the floor.

Nobody moved for what seemed to be several minutes.

"Coffee, anyone?" Lauren asked with forced cheerfulness.

"None for me, thanks." Mark looked at his watch. "Wow, I didn't know it was so late. I have to be going. Anybody need a ride?"

Susan spoke up quickly. "I do, if it's not too much trouble. My ride left earlier."

Celia looked back at the now silent Ouija

board. "I'll stay and help you clean up."

"There's no reason to do that," Lauren said in a rush. "I'll just put everything in the dishwasher and turn it on."

Celia couldn't disguise her look of relief. "If you're sure. I'll call you tomorrow."

"No phone yet, remember?" Lauren tried to keep her voice light. She had forgotten that she had no phone, and suddenly she didn't want them to leave just yet.

Robert was leaning on one of the wing-backed chairs beside the sofa, and he was still frowning. Lauren left him there and went to see the others out.

When she returned, she met Robert coming into the library. "Well, it's just the two of us," she said brightly. "Would you like that tour now?"

"Not tonight. It really is getting late."

"Since when is eleven-thirty late?" She took his hand and led him into the hall, but as she preceded him up the stairs, she noticed he didn't follow her. "Aren't you coming? I thought we could finish the tour in my bedroom—or better yet, in the blue room. There's a bed in there you'll have to see to believe."

The joints of the house creaked as if a gust of wind had touched it.

"I don't think this is the best time for that. We're both upset, and I can see you're tired."

"I'm not *that* tired. Robert, what's going on with you tonight? You've been like a caged bear all evening."

"I don't know. Maybe it's knowing you bought this house for us and never so much as asked my opinion. Maybe you don't like my house, but *I* do—and I'm not sure I want to move into a pile of lumber that looks like the house in *Psycho*. Maybe it's because I see you making all these plans and not bothering to see if I'm ready for these permanent steps or not."

Lauren came back to the bottom step. "What's that supposed to mean? Aren't we engaged? I assumed that implied permanent plans were the order of the day."

Robert looked away and shoved his hands into his pants pockets. "I don't think this is a good time to discuss it. Both of us are tired and our nerves are on edge."

"My nerves are just fine," she heatedly replied. "I've never seen you act like this, and I can't see any reason why you won't at least come see my upstairs rooms. Are you afraid the Ouija board will get you?"

"Don't talk like a fool!"

"A fool? You're right, Robert. It's time you left." Lauren stalked to the front door and jerked it open. Her angry eyes followed him out and into the night before she slammed the door and locked it.

She stormed through the downstairs turning off lights, too upset to bother cleaning up the mess. At the top of the stairs, she turned off the hall light, plunging the last of the downstairs into a well of darkness.

In her bedroom, Lauren stripped and carelessly tossed her clothes onto a chair. She was in no mood for neatness. She pulled on the first nightgown she found and yanked down the covers of her bed. Still fuming at Robert, she snapped off her bedside lamp.

Instantly, the room was cloaked in impenetrable blackness, and though her eyes were wide open, only her memory gave her a clue as to her surroundings. She thought this must be what it was like to become blind, and the notion was unnerving. Moments later, she felt relieved as her eyes adjusted and the furnishings in her room began to reappear, lit by the faint glow of moonlight coming through the window. Below her she heard the now familiar creaks and pops of the house settling for the night. She resolutely closed her eyes and willed herself to sleep.

Lauren wasn't sure what disturbed her sleep. For a minute she lay there, neither awake nor asleep. Something wasn't right. She opened her eyes and looked around the room. Everything was exactly as she had left it. What was different?

She listened and heard nothing, then realized it was the absence of any sound at all that was wrong. She strained to hear something, anything familiar, but heard nothing—not even the distant sounds of traffic or night insects or the hum of the various electrical appliances. Nothing at all.

Lauren sat up in bed and turned on the bedside lamp. When light filled the room, she knew the fuses hadn't blown. Thoroughly awake now, Lauren got out of bed and padded barefoot out to the foyer around the stairs.

Both below and above her, the steps led into an inky void that concealed everything beyond. Lauren frowned. She couldn't let herself be afraid of her own house. That was not only childish but ridiculous. She was about to go back to bed when she heard a faint noise far in the back of the house.

Her frown deepened into concern. Was someone down there? She listened again and heard the sound once more. There was no telephone to call the police. She looked around for a weapon and found a hammer on one of the window sills in her bedroom. Gripping it tightly, she drew a deep breath. She had to go down there.

Slowly, her bare feet silent on the steps, she went down into the blackness. She fought back the urge to turn on the lights. If she had a burglar, the darkness would be her cover.

At the landing she paused by the grandfather clock, then forced herself to go on. Holding the hammer in both hands she eased down to the ground floor.

In the hall she hesitated. She could run out the front door and to the safety of her neighbor's house, but she was barefoot and wearing only a thin nightgown. Also there was no guar-

antee the Barkers would be home. She might
be forced to return to the dark house and not
know if the intruder was upstairs or down.

Again she heard it, this time sure it had come
from the drawing room. It sounded as if someone were sitting in one of the wing-back chairs,
occasionally shifting his weight.

Moving as quietly as possible, Lauren crept
to the drawing room door. Her cold fingers
closed over the porcelain knob and twisted it.
Gingerly, she pushed the door back and peered
inside.

The room seemed empty. Moonlight coming
through the back windows silhouetted the wisteria's grotesque trunk, giving her a start before she recognized it for what it was. Both the
wing-back chairs faced the game table in the
corner of the room. She could see the chair on
the far side was empty, but the other faced
away from the door. As she stared, the sound
came again, and she would have screamed if
she had been able to breathe. Her throat was
constricted, and the icy chill of fear along her
spine had immobilized her. Her wide eyes
were fastened on the back of the chair nearest
the door.

Time lost all meaning as she wrestled with
the decision to run or stay and fight. At length
the latter won out. Gripping the hammer in
one hand, she inched her way down the wall,
her free hand in search of the light switch.

Abigail McDaniels

When she found it, she drew a steadying breath, raised the hammer and flooded the room with light.

The chair was empty.

Chapter Three

On Saturday Lauren went to the library and requested information on the history of her house. The young woman behind the counter, who looked as if she was fresh out of high school, gave Lauren a blank look.

"Four Seasons," Lauren explained again. "It was owned by a Mr. Nathaniel Padgett."

At last, understanding lit the girl's eyes. "Padgett. You want the genealogy records."

"No. I'm interested in the house, not the family who owned it."

"I'm sorry, but we don't have any records like that. Siddel Marsh is so small, we don't have much in the way of any records at all."

"Is there a historical society here?"

The girl shook her head.

Lauren sighed. "Surely you must have some sort of records that will tell me about the house."

"I could show you our newspapers on microfilm."

"I guess I could try that. How far back do they go?"

The girl brightened. "We have a complete set to 1899 and some partials that go back another ten years." With pride she led Lauren to the filing cabinets which contained the canisters of microfilm and instructed her on the use of the projector. "Don't reshelve the canisters," she cautioned. "We have to keep them in order."

Lauren selected the reel for 1910, the year her house was built. At once she was swept back into a world of Model T's, kerosene lanterns and kitchen pumps. She was so fascinated by the clothing styles that she almost forgot to look for her house.

There was no mention of Four Seasons at all. Not to be discouraged, Lauren began searching for the name of Nathaniel Padgett. This proved more profitable. The name seemed to leap at her off the yellow-brown page in the December issue.

"Mr. Nathaniel Padgett of Siddel Marsh has returned to town after a lengthy cruise. The sympathy of his friends and acquaintances go out to him over his recent bereavement."

Lauren reread the brief statement again. Evidently his wife or a parent had died—or perhaps a child. Infant mortality was higher earlier in the century. The realtor had said Padgett died when he was 100 years old. That would make him in his early twenties in 1910.

Idly Lauren searched back through the microfilm until she reached March. "Siddel Marsh's heart goes out to Mr. Nathaniel Padgett in the loss of his wife. Although Mrs. Padgett wasn't a long-term resident of this town, we will all miss her gentle smile and unselfish works. Mr. Padgett leaves Thursday next for Europe."

The gushy, nostalgic writing style brought a smile to Lauren's face. Newspaper reporting had come a long way. So it was his wife who had died. Childbirth, perhaps? The paper didn't say what the cause of death was, but Lauren suspected they naturally would have omitted something that personal. Victorian mores were still holding firm in Siddel Marsh even as late as 1910. She looked back at the date. March, 1910. Nathaniel couldn't have been too broken-hearted since he left immediately on a nine-month cruise.

Lauren cut off the projector and rewound the microfilm. She had thought men were more romantic then, but obviously Nathaniel Padgett hadn't fit that mold. Nor was he hurting for money if he could afford nine months in Europe to assuage his grief. To her surprise, she actually felt upset over him taking off on a vacation with his wife scarcely cold in her grave. She wondered if his contemporaries saw this as scandalous or if such trips were not uncommon at all.

As Lauren left the library, she felt vaguely disappointed. In a small town whose roots reached back to the French settlers of centuries ago, Lauren had expected to find reams of historical data.

What had begun as a whim was becoming important to her. She had hoped to find some mention of Four Season's interiors before she tackled the rooms upstairs. With such an odd theme and unique layout, she had assumed someone would have written an article about the house. At one time it must have been the grandest house in town.

Realizing it was already 12:30, Lauren hurried on home. She had received a call at her office the day before from the phone company informing her that the work on her new line was scheduled for the following day, sometime after noon. She had been told her presence at the house wouldn't be necessary until they got ready to do the inside work, but Lauren didn't trust the line men not to put one of their telephone poles where one of her ancient magnolias was.

She let herself in through the kitchen door and felt the house settle about her. That was one of the oddities of Four Seasons—it seemed to physically welcome her with the lemon-scented waxes and rose sachets and the subtle scent of clove.

For a moment she paused, again trying to

figure out exactly which of her cleaners had the aroma of cloves. The fragrance was almost like an old-fashioned shaving cream smell, one that triggered a childhood memory long forgotten but somehow poignant.

With ease, she wound her way through the now familiar maze of pantries and into the hall. Through the wide double doors at the far end of the hall, she could see the front parlor, which had been her first room to renovate. Now she wished she had done more research first, because the colors she had chosen were much too light for the way the house must have been designed. At the time she was doing the work, she had wanted brightness to dispel the gloom, but now she thought she might have gone too far.

Knowing the telephone man might not come for hours, Lauren decided to read for a while and enjoy her day off. She went to her room and looked on the nightstand where she always left the current book she was reading. It was bare.

Puzzled, Lauren looked around the room and even felt beneath the bedcovers in case she had inadvertently made up the bed with the book inside. It was nowhere in the room.

Lauren sighed with frustration. She rarely lost things, and when she did she couldn't rest until they were retrieved.

After a thorough search of the house, she had to admit defeat. That left her with nothing to do but watch television. She turned on the set but could find nothing except sports shows and cartoons, so she turned it off and meandered from room to room, trying to find something of interest to do.

At the door to the library, she paused and looked behind her. No one was there, of course, so she continued on into the dark paneled room. Most of the books there were exactly as Nathaniel Padgett had left them. Some were amusingly old, such as a classroom reader featuring impossibly perfect children, or the impressive *Manning's Horse Book* for do-it-yourself veterinarian work. There were volumes of poetry with age-darkened, gold-embossed spines, but Lauren had never cared much for poetry. She liked novels, the sexier the better, and there were none of those at all in this library. The newest book of any kind was almost 30 years old.

As she sat on the window seat, thumbing through the pages, she discovered the book dealt with the subject of reincarnation. "Give me a break," she muttered. "One life is enough."

She shelved the book and wandered into the drawing room. The scent of cloves wafted to her. Since that night when she had been so sure someone was sitting in one of the wing-back chairs, she had felt vaguely uneasy in this room. She assumed her apprehension was because she had behaved so foolishly that night. Thank goodness no one had seen her. If she had given in to her impulses and raced in her nightgown to the neighbors, she would have died of embarrassment.

Lauren glanced over her shoulder, thinking she had heard something behind her, only to find the doorway empty. Nonsense, she thought as she moved to the opposite side of the room and turned so her back was not to the doorway. She glanced at the Ouija board on the game table she was standing beside, then looked away. She wished Susan had never given it to her. They weren't close friends, and the apparent extravagance of the gift made it inappropriate. Besides, Lauren disliked superstitions such as this and didn't believe in them at all. The best thing to do would be to put it out of sight and forget about it. Surely Susan wouldn't be so rude as to ask where it was when she came to visit—*if* she came. Lauren wasn't at all sure she wanted to encourage a friendship with such an odd person.

Still, the board was well-made—a work of art, really. It looked pretty on the polished top of the game table. She picked it up and turned it over to examine the back. A fancifully intertwined N. S. P. seemed to float on the walnut board in mother-of-pearl inlay.

Lauren traced her finger over the letters. N. S. P.? Surely it couldn't stand for Nathaniel S. Padgett. That would be too coincidental.

With her curiosity brimming, she hurried into the library and pulled out a child's primer. There on the cover page was written "Nathaniel Syler Padgett" in a child's wavering script.

She snapped the book shut. Susan had said the Ouija board was part of an estate sale. The realtor had told her that all the personal articles had been disposed of in that way. It seemed one of the estate items had found its way home again.

Lauren went back to the drawing room and gazed down at the board. Her new knowledge of it made it seem that much more eerie, but at the same time made it a great conversation piece. She decided to leave it where it was, at least for the time being.

Restless and bored and unable to find the book she wanted to read, she decided she might as well do some cleaning. Armed with dust rags from one of the pantries, she moved through the dining room, lifting candlesticks to dust under them then rubbing her finger smudges off the silver surfaces. Twice she thought she heard someone come in and looked up to find no one. Lauren disliked waiting for repairmen, or anyone else, for that matter. And she hated being idle. It made her too imaginative.

Her mother had always warned her about her imagination. Imagination had been the downfall of her Aunt Mabel, and it almost had been the downfall of Lauren herself. That had been a long time ago, she told herself as the floorboards creaked behind her. Years ago. She wasn't sure what caused Aunt Mabel to lose her grip on reality, but Lauren blamed her own past problem on being too overworked in college. Her mother had been equally sure her imagination was to blame. At any rate, Lauren had suffered what her mother always referred to as a nervous breakdown, but she was well now. She had been well for years.

In the parlor, Lauren ran the dust rag over the mantel's elaborate carvings, even though, for some reason, it never seemed to need dusting. For the first time, she noticed what appeared to be initials, intertwined in the other carving. After studying the pattern for a minute and exercising a bit of poetic license, she was sure she could see an N and an L forming the background for a P. It couldn't be an L, she reasoned. An S for Syler was much more logical, but it didn't look like an S. She had to smile at the old man's family pride. He seemed to have put his initials on everything.

Behind her in the entry hall she heard a thud that sounded as if someone had dropped something. "Hello?" she called out as she gripped her dust rag and tried to keep her voice from quivering. "Who's there?"

When she heard nothing she cautiously went into the hallway. It was empty, and the doors leading to the other rooms were shut, just as she had left them. However, in the middle of the floor was a book.

Lauren hesitated and glanced around again. That book couldn't possibly have been there minutes before or she would have seen it. Cautiously she went to it and picked it up. It was her book, the one she had searched for but couldn't find.

A shiver ran up her spine, and she looked up the stairs to the dim heights far above.

At that instant, the doorbell peeled, and she jumped. Through the etched and frosted pane of the front door she saw a man in the distinctive blue uniform of the telephone company. Feeling foolish at having been startled, Lauren went to the door and opened it.

"Phone man," he said. "I'm here to put in your line. Got a dog?"

"No." She wondered if she should admit that to a stranger. She suddenly felt alone and vulnerable. "Were you . . . were you here earlier? Here in this hall a few minutes ago?"

"No, ma'am." He gave her a peculiar look. "We never enter a house without the owner being present. Company policy."

Lauren shook her head. Of course he hadn't been. No one had been. That had been her imagination. "Where will you put the new phone line?"

He took her around the house and pointed in her neighbor's direction. "I'll bring a line through here and put a pole there on the fence line, just this side." He gestured at the turret window. "Connect up there. Be through by midafternoon. Can call your friends tonight." He grinned.

Lauren wondered if he was capable of putting in a phone when he didn't seem able to form complete sentences. "An overhead line?

I had assumed it would be underground."

"No, ma'am. Not in this section of town. In the new houses, maybe."

"Okay." There was no point in arguing with the man. Unsightly lines or not, she needed a telephone.

She went back inside and looked again at her book and at the spot where she had found it. Why had it sounded as if the book had fallen from several feet up in the air? Again she peered up at the empty stairwell.

Lauren left the book in the parlor while she methodically resumed dusting. Once she started something, she never stopped until it was finished.

In only 20 minutes, she was settling down in the parlor with her book. The floors above her head creaked and popped, drawing her attention to the ceiling. No one was up there, she reassured herself. She was positive of that. She began to read.

Hours later Lauren lowered the book to turn a page and saw the repair man standing directly in front of her. She gasped in fright.

"Ma'am? I said, where do you want the phone?"

"How did you get in here?"

"The front door was open. I thought you said for me to come in." He looked as uncomfortable as she felt.

A shiver ran through her. "Did you knock? I never heard you knock." All the horror stories she had ever heard of rape and murder were racing through her mind.

"Where do you want the phone? About quitting time. Like to finish up if I can."

Lauren eased cautiously out of the chair and was relieved to see him retreat a couple of paces. "Here. On this wall." She stared at him, her fear not quite dispelled. "And another one upstairs in my bedroom. It's the room with yellow walls." She wasn't about to go upstairs with him.

"I can do this one, but I don't have a work order for two phone jacks."

"But I need two—one upstairs and one down. I thought that was understood."

He reached into his pocket and pulled out a work order. After scowling at it a moment he shook his head. "It's not on here. I didn't bring out enough wire to put in two. Can call tomorrow and request another one."

Lauren made an effort to control her temper. This wasn't the first time she had come in contact with Siddel Marsh's inefficiency. "All right. Put in the one down here."

"I can wait if you want both of them at once."

"No, no. I'd like to have at least the one now."

She backed away as he knelt on the floor to start drilling the necessary holes. Had he knocked or was he just saying that? Surely she would have heard him if he had knocked. Lau-

ren put her fingertips to her temples where a
headache was forming.

Keeping one eye on the workman she went
to the door and looked down the hall at the
front door. It was standing wide open. Of
course, she thought, the workman could have
left it like that. She considered shutting it but
decided she felt better with it open.

She went back to her chair and picked up
her book. There was no way she would be able
to concentrate on it with the man making so
much noise, but she wanted to keep an eye on
him and felt awkward about openly staring.

"Never been in here before."

"I beg your pardon?" She tried to look as if
she had been engrossed in the story and resented the interruption.

"Never been inside before," he repeated
cheerfully. "Knew Old Man Padgett by sight,
of course. Everybody did."

Lauren looked back down at the page.

"Never thought it would sell, 'specially not
to a single woman."

"Why not?" she asked coolly. How did he
know she was unmarried?

He shrugged and drilled a hole before he
added, "Stories go around, you know."

"No, I don't know."

"Old Man Padgett, he was a weird one. You
know what I mean. Always kept to himself.
Only came out when he had to buy something
to eat so he wouldn't starve."

Lauren reluctantly closed her book. She

might not like making conversation with him, but perhaps he could tell her something about the house. "At his age I assumed he was in a rest home for the last years of his life."

"Not him. You couldn't have blasted him out of here."

"Someone must have looked in on him from time to time. Surely he wasn't completely alone."

The man chuckled. "He sure wouldn't have liked that. Not at all."

"How sad that he was so alone. Surely there must be some family of his somewhere."

"Nope. Neither kith nor kin as they say."

Lauren frowned. "No friends even?"

"No friends for sure. Didn't want any. Outlived the ones he might have had earlier."

"Are you saying he never went anywhere or had anyone over to visit?"

"That's right. He was real odd. Always said he was waiting for her to come back—his wife, that is."

"Did she?" Lauren found she was holding her breath.

"Shoot no. She died. Right after they was married."

"You mean he married only once? If she was dead how could he expect her to come back? That doesn't make any sense."

"You're telling me. I said he was weird." He began fitting the wires into the wall.

Lauren felt cold all over. She hadn't wanted to hear this. The man who had lived here for eighty years was crazy? "Maybe there was a second wife, one you don't know about, one who deserted him."

"Nope. Old Man Padgett is a legend around here. He just had one 'wife, and she's over to the cemetery."

"Are you almost through?" Lauren wanted him to finish and leave. She thought he must be trying to frighten her for some reason. Why else would he have sneaked into the parlor as he did? She wondered if she should call the office and report him.

"Just about."

She sat in silence while he put the phone jack into place and plugged in the white phone she had ordered. He made a call to check out the line and had them dial back to make sure the phone rang properly. The sound of the bell seemed to resound in the house. Lauren looked around as if the sound were alien to her.

"That's it." He stood and nodded decisively. "You want that other line run, call the office tomorrow."

She nodded. She wasn't at all sure she wanted to take a chance on having the same workman show up.

She let him out the door and locked it behind him, double-checking to be sure it was secure. How had he appeared before her without her even knowing he had come in the house? Usually every footstep seemed unusually loud on the oak floors. Her own steps did as she went to the stairs. The floorboards even creaked behind her as if someone else had followed her. She looked thoughtfully back at the empty hall.

Was it this peculiarity of the house that had made the poor old man think his dead wife was there? If he was already mentally unstable, it might have been a possibility.

But the workman had said Padgett expected her to "come back." Not that he thought she had already returned. Lauren shook her head. She had enough trouble quelling her own imagination without trying to understand that of a dead man. He was insane or had become senile, and of the two, she chose to believe the latter.

Chapter Four

"Are you really happy here?" Celia asked as she and Lauren sat drinking coffee on the back porch.

"Of course I am. I love this house." She avoided Celia's eyes and gazed at the twisted trunk of the wisteria. Beyond the yard lay the swamp and a glimpse of the lake, both shrouded in a hazy mist.

"But it's so big for only one person. I should think you'd be lonely out here."

"Not really." Lauren put her coffee cup on the wicker table and said, "At first I was, though I wouldn't admit it, but now it's as if the house has always been mine. I can't really explain it. Haven't you ever been some place and felt instantly at home?"

"Like déjà vu?"

"More than that. More as if you ... belong there."

"No."

"Like I said, I can't explain it. This house just suits me." She laughed self-consciously. "It was love at first sight."

"I've always heard love is blind," Celia teased with a laugh. "Actually I like what you've done with it downstairs. When will you start on the second floor?"

"Soon, I suppose." Lauren looked out at the still water that circled the base of the silent cypress trees beyond her yard. She found the swamp so calming. "There's really no hurry."

"I'd have done my bedroom right away if it were me. Those dark colors are so oppressive."

Lauren snapped her head around. "Not to me."

"I don't mean to upset you. After all, it's your house."

"Some people find dark colors more restful."

Celia gave her an odd look. "I suppose so."

For a few moments neither spoke, then Lauren broke the silence. "The telephone repairman told me about Mr. Padgett. You know, the man who owned this house?"

"Oh? What did he say?"

"It seems he was a bit peculiar in his old age. His wife died young, and he always expected her to come back." Lauren hummed the opening bars from *The Twilight Zone*. "Picture, if you will, an old man—lonely, depressed, in need of a friend. A man who misses his wife and who will find her again . . . in *The Twilight Zone*."

Celia laughed with her. "Mark told me something about that."

Lauren's smile faded. "He did? And you didn't tell me?"

"I didn't think it was important. The man is dead and buried, and you aren't superstitious. Besides, Robert told you the old man had the reputation of being weird."

"I thought he meant eccentric or senile, not crazy. Don't you think it sounds crazy to expect a dead wife to come back?"

"It's not the most sane thing I've ever heard, but maybe he was so much in love with her that he couldn't bear to think he would never see her again."

"For eighty years?"

"I don't know. If he had enough money to build and maintain this place, I suspect he was rich enough to be considered eccentric. Even at the turn of the century this place must have cost a fortune."

"It's not quite that old. It dates from 1910."

"Same difference as far as I'm concerned."

Lauren frowned. "You know, something happened the day the phone was installed that has worried me a bit."

"Oh?"

"I lost my book. I looked everywhere for it. Then I heard a sound like something had fallen, and when I went into the hall, there it was—right in the middle of the floor."

"You must have dropped it when you went downstairs," Celia said with a shrug.

"No, that's not possible. In the first place, I left it upstairs by my bed, and in the second, I would certainly have noticed if I had dropped it. Besides, I had been through the hall several times, and it wasn't there."

"Obviously you overlooked it."

"And when I started reading it, I lost all track of time. I looked up and found the telephone man standing right in front of me."

"In the house? They aren't supposed to come in without knocking."

"He said he did and he thought I called out for him to come in, but I didn't."

"He must have lied. You ought to report him."

"I guess I should have. On top of everything else, he only had enough equipment to install the phone in the parlor. I distinctly asked for an extension upstairs. I *know* I did."

"You know how this phone company is. He probably forgot to put it on the truck and didn't want to go back after it, or whoever took down the order screwed it up."

"I'm sure that's true, but I've been reluctant to call about the extension for fear they'll send the same man back out. He was creepy, the way he just showed up in front of me like that."

"As small as Siddel Marsh is, he may be the only man they have to do installations." Celia grinned. "Maybe he swiped your book and was doing some quick reading instead of working."

Lauren managed to smile. "I'm not sure he's capable of reading."

Celia took another sip of her coffee. "How did we ever end up in this town anyway? I mean, I landed here after a divorce, but I could have moved away like my ex-husband did."

"I was offered a job at Newton and Combe and saw it as a chance to work my way up in a small company. Newton retires next year, and Combe is only a couple of years younger. Robert is being groomed to take Newton's place, and I'll be an obvious choice for his partner when Combe is gone. Not many architects have their own company while still in their thirties. Besides, I thought Siddel Marsh was picturesque. I still do."

Celia nodded. "Mark and I are dating pretty steadily these days. I guess my chances of escaping this town are dwindling. He's lived here all his life and thinks there's no other place on earth for him."

"Working in the family business is a sure way to the top."

"Mark is a good accountant," Celia said, loyally defending him. "He could be a success anywhere."

"I didn't mean to imply otherwise."

"You and Robert do plan to get married, don't you? You've dated for such a long while. What has it been? Six or seven years?"

Lauren frowned. "I don't know. Yes, probably." She knew she shouldn't have said anything Celia could construe as derogatory about Mark's abilities. They both knew Mark was mediocre at best. "Yes, I'm sure we'll get married."

"Does Robert like the house?"

"It will grow on him. You know how he likes chrome and glass. Antiques are more my long suit." She paused. "We'll work it out."

Celia looked away, her eyes following the lake's grassy shore line. "Have you seen Susan lately?"

"Only at work. We aren't really friends."

"No? I thought you were since she gave you such an expensive housewarming gift."

"Since she's the only secretary at Newton and Combe we're on friendly terms, but that's all." Lauren glanced at Celia. "I felt uncomfortable about her giving it to me. Why do you suppose she did it?"

"I don't know. She's a strange one."

"Did I tell you what I found on the back of it? The initials N. S. P. I think it stands for Nathaniel Syler Padgett. How about that for weird?"

"Are you sure? It belonged to Old Man Padgett?"

"Maybe. Susan said the antique dealer got it from the liquidation of someone's estate, and how many estates could there be in Siddel Marsh where the initials would be N. S. P? I don't know what to make of it."

Celia shrugged. "It's a strange coincidence, that's all. Like the story in the paper not long ago about a man who lost his class ring while he was fishing and years later he caught the fish that swallowed it. That was stranger than Susan buying a Ouija board that was part of this original estate. Like you say, it's a small town."

"I guess." Lauren finished her coffee and put the cup on the table. "More coffee?"

"No, thanks. It's getting late, and I ought to be going. Mark is taking me out to eat this evening, and I need to change clothes. Besides, there's a fog forming over the lake, and I don't want to get caught driving in it."

Lauren looked at the pewter-hued water that reflected the overcast skies above. As Celia had said, tendrils of fog were floating just above the slick surface and blending up into the mist. "It looks more like a winter evening than spring."

"We've had peculiar weather this whole year."

They carried the coffee cups into the kitchen, and Lauren led the way to the hall through the series of pantries.

"How do you find your way about in here? I'd get lost for sure."

"I'm thinking about taking out some of the dividing walls. A butler's pantry and keeping room and whatever storage the other two were used for might have been fashionable in 1910, but I have no use for them."

"If it were me, I'd make one long room and simplify everything."

"Maybe I will."

Celia paused at the front door. "Are you sure you're okay out here?"

"Of course I am."

"I know how stubborn you are. Would you admit it if you regretted having bought this place? No one would think anything about it if you decided to sell it and get something more conventional."

"Nonsense," Lauren said with a laugh. "I love it here."

"Okay. Give me a call next week, and we'll have dinner."

"Sure." Lauren closed the door behind her friend. From far away up the stairs the faint sound of another door being shut drifted down. Lauren glanced up the stairwell but didn't bother to investigate. She was becoming accustomed to the house's odd echoes and unexpected sounds.

She walked back to the kitchen by the circuitous route of the formal parlor, library and drawing room. As her feet crossed oak floor, rugs and more oak flooring her footsteps sounded, faded and sounded again.

She turned on the light in the kitchen to dispel the shadows which were already thick in its corners and recesses, then washed the coffee cups before making supper. All her life she had had an aversion to leaving dirty dishes sitting about.

Because of the contrast between the bright interior light and the rapidly fading daylight outside, the kitchen window was filled with darkness, and she avoided looking at it. Anyone outside this window or the ones overlooking the porch could see her clearly. She had decided against putting up blinds in order to maintain the house's character, but she wasn't sure now that her decision had been correct.

By the time Lauren got around to preparing something to eat, her edginess had displaced most of her appetite, so she decided on a simple salad. As she searched the refrigerator for dressing, she thought she heard something and stopped to listen. It had sounded like the footsteps of someone walking across the rug in the adjoining drawing room.

She held herself motionless for a time, but there was nothing to hear. With a shake of her head, she finished making her salad and went out onto the porch and sat in one of the wicker chairs to eat.

Though the air was heavy with mist, the soft evening light gave the surrounding marsh and lake a gauzy, surrealistic appearance. Like a watercolor Poe might have painted, she thought with some amusement. The mist and fog blurred the lines of trees and garage and the wall of the house that rounded about the turret—an effect that was both romantic and mysterious. She found herself wishing Robert were here. This was a perfect night for making love.

She was surprised at her thoughts. She and Robert occasionally spent the night together at his house, or had before she had become so

Abigail McDaniels

involved in restoring this house, but their liaisons had never been overly romantic. Robert was much too pragmatic for flowery speeches, and she had always thought them silly herself. Their lack of sentimentality in personal relationships and their dedication to their work were two things she and Robert had in common.

The fog that curled off the water and threaded through the low bushes that bounded the swamp was almost luminescent in the gloaming. Lauren tried to recall if she had ever before seen fog and mist at the same time, but she wasn't sure. She wasn't the outdoors type, and weather conditions weren't one of her strong interests.

As she watched through the gathering darkness, an arm of the fog floated toward the garage as if its intent was to caress the mellow bricks of the structure. The sight was fascinating, even hypnotizing. The sweet scent of wisteria drifted to Lauren, and she inhaled deeply of its fragrant aroma. Suddenly, she was pulled from her reverie by the realization that the smell could only have come from her imagination. The wisteria had finished blooming days ago.

Ignoring the remainder of her salad, she strolled across the porch and put her hand on the gnarled wisteria trunk. By leaning out over the rail and looking up, she could see it twist and bend up the back of the house and about the turret. Now that the clusters of flowers were gone, the vines were covered with a dense growth of leaves. Her imagination still supplied the cloying scent, but this time she chose to enjoy it.

With darkness fast approaching, she could barely make out the outline of the top of the fog-shrouded turret. Her face felt moist from the warm mist, and again she wished Robert were there, holding her in the softness of the night.

Lauren shook the fancy from her head and went inside, picking up her plate as she passed the table. If she kept this up, she would become as odd as old Nathaniel Padgett had been.

She washed and dried the plate, then again wiped clean the already spotless countertops, hoping the mundane chore would help her curb her overly creative thoughts. But the hollow, reverberating plunking wouldn't go away. When she had first heard it, she thought it was the kitchen faucet dripping, but a glance had told her the source of the noise was elsewhere. At two- or three-second intervals, the plunk came again. Almost certain this was not her imagination, she moved about the room, listening to see if the sound became louder or softer. As she stepped toward the old well in the back of the kitchen, the plunk became more distinct. Then the obvious became apparent to her, and she felt foolish for not having immediately thought of the well as the source. Clearly the dripping she was hearing was from

Abigail McDaniels

condensation forming on the inside of the well cover.

Since moving in, she had paid little attention to the well, assuming it was dry and probably filled with rubble, but droplets of condensation wouldn't have formed if the well were dry. With her curiosity piqued, she set aside the old well bucket that she had decorated with an arrangement of silk flowers and opened the cover against the creaking protest of its aged hinges.

The light from the kitchen only illuminated the first few feet of the well's slick, rock-lined interior. Beyond that was nothing but blackness. She heard another plunk, this time much louder now that the cover was open.

Lauren got a flashlight from a kitchen drawer and leaned over the edge for a better look. Far below, she saw an oily reflection of the light and her own silhouette. The well still had water in it, and for some reason this amazed her. Then she remembered her proximity to the lake. Of course the well had water—lake water. There was nothing strange about that.

A shiver ran through her as she studied the water so far below and the sheer sides of the well. If she fell in, she would never be able to climb back out. Vertigo gripped her as her imagination put her in the well, screaming and drowning in its slimy depths.

With a gasp Lauren pushed away from the well, gripping the flashlight as if it were a lifeline. She was trembling from head to toe, and it took an extreme act of will for her to step near enough to slam the well cover again. The sound crashed around her and reverberated throughout the house.

Hastily Lauren pushed the bucket of flowers back in place. Once again her imagination had attacked her. She hadn't had a panic attack like this in years—not since her junior year in college, to be exact, the time her mother referred to as her breakdown.

Lauren backed away from the well and out of the kitchen. She couldn't bring herself to turn off the light or to pass through the maze of pantries. At the drawing room door she bolted for the library and with shaking fingers turned on the light switch.

The accustomed appearance of the room had a calming effect. Everything was normal; everything was in its place. She wasn't in any danger. As she had learned to do in the past, Lauren sat in a chair and took slow, steady breaths until the pounding of her heart subsided. She was safe. She wasn't going to fall into the well. Over and over again she repeated the litany of calming thoughts. This was only a minor setback. It wasn't an indication of her old trouble returning.

When she was perfectly calm, Lauren went upstairs to get ready for bed. Her house was quiet about her, quiet and peaceful. She felt its protection and the security of walls that had stood strong for 80 years. She was safe here.

By the time she finished her bath and put

on her gown, Lauren was chastizing herself for becoming so afraid. It had only been an anxiety attack, one such as many people suffered daily. She should be glad she had them so rarely. In fact she hadn't had one of this magnitude since college. Luckily no one else had witnessed her unreasoning terror.

Leaving the bathroom light on, she turned off her bedroom light and drew aside her window curtains so she could gaze out at the night. The sky had cleared, and moonlight dispersing throughout the blanket of mist cast the world about her in a silvery glow. The fog below seemed to slowly writhe and undulate with sensuous movements as it floated across the lawn. This was a night for making love.

She glanced at her bedside clock. It was still early. Robert would be up, probably watching the evening news. It would be easy to call him and ask him to come over.

With a smile Lauren padded barefoot downstairs. Below her feet lay the darkness, but she was unafraid. She was safe in this house.

In the hall she turned on the light so she could locate the parlor door, and as she crossed to the phone, she told herself she really had to ask for the extension to be installed. This was altogether too inconvenient an arrangement.

After settling herself on the sofa, with her feet curled beneath her, she dialed Robert's number. His phone rang numerous times, and she was on the verge of hanging up when he finally answered. "Robert, this is Lauren.

What took you so long to answer the phone?"

"Lauren? Is something wrong?"

"No, of course not. I was sort of lonely and thought I'd give you a call." Her voice was sultry with seduction.

There was a long pause before he answered. "Do you have any idea what time it is?"

"It's ten o'clock."

"Wrong. It's after midnight."

Lauren's smile faded. "It can't be. I know it's only ten. I looked at my clock before coming down to call you."

Robert sighed as if he wished he were still asleep. "You woke me up. I'm looking at my clock, and I know what time it is. Are you sure you're okay?"

"Of course I am." She cradled the receiver on her shoulder and wound the cord around her finger. "Would you like to come over?"

"Now?"

"Of course now, silly."

"Lauren, I don't know what this is all about, but it's late. I was already asleep."

"You're awake now."

"Only until I hang up this phone."

"Why don't you come over? I'm wearing my pink nightgown." She smiled because she knew it was his favorite.

After a moment Robert said, "I appreciate the offer, but you know I have a busy day tomorrow. The Brileys's blueprints are due at his lawyer's office before noon, and I've got a few last-minute changes to make."

"I know, but that's tomorrow and this is to-night." She lowered her voice to a husky note. "By the time you get here I could be wearing nothing at all."

"Are you drunk? What's going on over there?"

"Of course I'm not drunk," she said indignantly. "Nothing at all is going on over here. That's why I called you. Are you going to come over or not?"

"Good-bye, Lauren. I'm going back to sleep."

"Robert!"

"See you at work tomorrow."

She heard a click and knew he had hung up. Angrily she slammed down the receiver. He had turned her down.

She stood and went to the mirror across from the fireplace and glared at her reflection. Was she getting old? Her golden brown hair was mussed but not unattractively so. She was pale, but that made her eyes greener—or so Robert had always told her. Doubtfully, she touched her cheek. She was 35 but that wasn't old, and most of the time she looked younger than her years. The pink nightgown wasn't sheer, but it was flattering to her slender body. Why had Robert turned her down? And what was that malarkey about it being after midnight?

She went into the hall and crossed to the drawing room. The mantel clock there read 12:20.

Lauren stared at it. How had she lost two

hours? Her bedroom clock must have the wrong time, she decided. She made a mental note to reset it when she went upstairs.

Despite the lateness of the hour, she wasn't sleepy. No television stations were on the air in Siddel Marsh at that hour, and the library had no titles that interested her. The book she was reading was up in her bedroom, but Lauren didn't want to go back up yet.

Instead, she idly wandered over to the game table and sat down in front of the Ouija board. Carelessly she poked at the planchette. Robert could have been more tactful, she thought peevishly. Most fiancés would be glad to rush to their lover's bed. Maybe in the past seven years Robert's interest in her had cooled. Maybe he didn't really want to marry her, and she was kidding herself to think that he did.

Out of boredom she put the Ouija board on her lap as she had seen it done on television and rested her fingertips on the planchette.

"Tell me, o spirits from beyond," she said in a melodramatic voice, "is Robert my own true love or not?"

All at once the planchette began to swing wildly from side to side.

Lauren's eyes widened, and her mouth dropped open. She tried to hold the piece of wood still, but it only swung in wider arcs. Suddenly it leaped off the board, its momentum carrying it to the fireplace where it clattered onto the hearth. The clattering bounced off the walls and up the stairwell to echo far above her.

Lauren backed out of the chair and felt behind her for the door, not daring to take her eyes off the planchette or the Ouija board that had fallen to the floor at her feet.

Once in the hall, Lauren began to run, and she didn't slow down until she was in her bedroom, leaning against her bolted door. Her breath came in ragged gasps and burned her lungs. She was nauseated from fear, and her skin was clammy.

When she finally got herself under control, she looked at her bedside clock. It read 12:35, a time not inconsistent with the minutes she had spent in the drawing room. Her breath seemed to lodge in her throat. Somehow, between deciding to call Robert and dialing his number, she had lost two hours. As bile rose in her throat, Lauren ran for the bathroom.

Chapter Five

Lauren gave the waiter time to leave the table before she smiled across at Robert. "I'm glad we drove to Shreveport. There really isn't a decent place to eat in Siddel Marsh."

"I thought you liked the Shamrock Arms."

"It's all right for lunch, but it's not nearly as elegant as this place." Lauren looked around at the dimly lit room with its snowy tablecloths and crimson carpet. "I like going to nice places."

Robert made no comment.

After a while she said, "You're being awfully quiet tonight. Is something wrong?"

"No, nothing's wrong."

She smiled again and hugged herself. "I've had a wonderful day. I landed the Harrison project, and my sketches for the Wilsons's house were approved. Wait until you and I are the heads of the company! We'll design buildings like Siddel Marsh never heard of."

Robert gave her a peculiar look. "What do you mean by that?"

"Why, everybody knows Mr. Newton will retire any day now, and Mr. Combe is right behind him. You're being groomed to step in as full partner when Newton leaves, and who else would you pick to fill Combe's place but me?"

Before Robert could answer, the waiter arrived with their salads, and Lauren waited in silence for him to leave. She had always disliked airing her private conversations before strangers. As the waiter twisted the pepper mill over their salads, Lauren planned her future.

When they were alone again she said, "I think we should use the Winter room as the master suite."

"I beg your pardon?"

"My house—I think the blue bedroom would be best for us. It's always been the master bedroom and has the best view of the lake." She giggled girlishly. "And it has a *huge* bed."

"Lauren, I—"

"It adjoins the yellow room which we could use for a nursery. Of course it's much too large for one, but that can't be helped. Most houses have the opposite problem."

Robert's forehead puckered with a frown.

"What's the matter? Did I say something wrong?"

"It's just that you're planning our entire life. Don't I have any say in it?"

"Of course you do," she said with quick compassion as she reached out to take his hand. "Which room do you prefer for a nursery?"

Robert pulled away. "I think we're jumping the gun a bit, don't you?"

"Well, I hate to mention it, but neither of us are spring chickens, as they say in Siddel Marsh. If we're going to have a family, it should be right away."

"Don't you think we should get married first?"

Lauren laughed and poked coyly at her salad. "You're right."

"We haven't even set a wedding date yet."

She leaned forward expectantly. "When would be good for you?"

Robert glanced around as if he didn't want to be overheard. "I don't know. There's no rush, after all."

Lauren looked puzzled. "Not a rush, certainly, but you just agreed that—"

"No, I didn't agree to anything."

She cast her eyes down to her plate and ate some of her salad as she pondered his words. "I don't know what you're getting at. Don't you want to have children? You've always said you did."

Obviously exasperated, he put down his fork and said, "Look, Lauren, don't pressure me.

You're trying to put words into my mouth and coerce me into agreeing to things that I need more time to consider."

Lauren straightened. "I am? Such as?"

"Skip it. How's your salad?"

"Fine, thank you." As she picked at her salad, she glanced at him out of the corners of her eyes but said nothing.

When the steaks were brought to the table, Lauren discovered hers was too well-done, but since Robert was already in a bad mood and she didn't want him to have to wait even longer for his own steak, she chose not to send it back. Reluctantly, she took a bite and found the meat as flavorless as she had expected.

"Would you prefer me not to do that room in blue?" she ventured again. "I thought you liked that color. It carries the theme of the house, but I'll change it if you like."

"There you go again. Lauren, I don't even like that house. Why should I care what color you paint any of the rooms in it?"

Lauren's second bite of meat was even drier than the bite before. With difficulty, Lauren swallowed. "I assumed you'd care what color room we live in. I'm sorry if that assumption was incorrect," she added caustically.

"Look," Robert hissed, leaning forward and pitching his voice low so as not to be overheard by those at the adjoining tables, "I don't like that house, I don't want to live in that house, and I don't want to discuss that house. Understand?"

"Perfectly." Lauren found she couldn't eat the meat after all. "Waiter?" When he came to the table she said, "My meat is too well-done. I ordered rare."

"Yes, ma'am, but this is—"

Lauren interrupted. "Don't argue, please. Just take it away and fix it." '

Robert glared at her. "There was nothing wrong with that meat. You've already eaten most of it."

"Only a bite. I ought to know if it's cooked properly or not."

Robert put down his fork to wait for her meal to be returned.

"No, you go ahead," she said stiffly. "Don't wait for me."

"Nonsense. Of course I'll wait."

They sat in stiff silence until another steak was placed before her. Lauren cut into it and nodded a dismissal at the waiter.

"I don't see any difference between that one and the other," Robert observed.

"I think it's obvious. This one is rare and the other one was practically burnt."

Robert began to eat again, clearly trying to ignore her. But a few minutes later, after an awkward glance at her, he said, "You know, you've changed lately."

"I have? In what way?"

"I'm not sure. You're just different."

"I'm wearing a new perfume. Maybe that's it."

"I thought it was different."

91

"It's called 'Wisteria.' Do you like it?"

"Not as well as the one you usually wear."

"Thanks a lot," she said dryly.

"Well, you asked. I wasn't going to say anything otherwise."

Lauren sighed. That was so typical of Robert. He would have let her wear a perfume he didn't like rather than bother to discuss it. She wondered what else he objected to but had failed to mention. "Do you like my hair?"

He looked at the top of her head. "Are you wearing it differently? Looks the same to me."

"It is the same. I was only wondering if you like it."

"Sure."

She wasn't certain she believed him. He hadn't sounded very convincing. Maybe she should let it grow out and put it in a clip like some of the younger women at the office wore theirs. Younger. The word had slipped into her mind by a side entrance and refused to leave. She wasn't as young as she once was. Lauren put down her fork.

"What's wrong now?"

"Nothing. I'm not hungry."

"After sending the steak back and getting another one you aren't going to eat it?"

"That was the cook's fault, not mine. We paid for this meat to be properly cooked, and if I choose not to eat it that's my business."

Robert laid down his fork and motioned for the check.

Lauren stared off into space, refusing to

meet the waiter's eyes or to acknowledge Robert's presence. When the bill was paid, she stood and regally swept out of the restaurant.

At the car, she waited for Robert to open her door, then slid into the passenger seat. She had always liked this car. It reminded her of a black carriage she had once seen and admired. Lauren frowned. Where had that thought come from? She couldn't recall ever having seen a black carriage, and Robert's new-model Buick didn't resemble one at all. She put her fingertips to her temple and rubbed at the headache that was forming.

Although he seemed reluctant, Robert got in behind the wheel, and they drove out into the night. The darkness had an unreal quality to Lauren, as if it were stage scenery or a painted curtain that could be ripped open to expose a different world. Her headache was increasing rapidly. She closed her eyes and forced herself to take measured breaths and to relax all her muscles. She hated and feared the migraines that put her in bed, sometimes for days on end.

When her headache at last began to subside, Lauren opened her eyes, surprised to find they were entering Siddel Marsh. "That was a quick ride home," she commented.

"Was it? I thought it seemed longer than usual."

So Robert intended to be perverse, she thought. Well, let him.

Lauren stared out her window as Robert turned off the highway and headed through the darkest residential section of town. Although this way was shorter, Lauren always avoided driving through this neighborhood at night because it was so poorly lit. Robert was usually considerate in avoiding it as well when she was with him, but tonight he was obviously in a hurry. Several minutes later, Lauren breathed a sigh of relief as they passed through the sleepy downtown area. Although all its stores were locked and dimmed for the night, the streets were well lit and the buildings were familiar. The corner where the feed store had once stood was now a dress shop with one of those cutesy-clever names that seemed inherent to small towns. The livery stable had long since been torn down and was now a parking area. The old bank had been renovated to keep up with the changing times. Lauren rubbed the bridge of her nose and wished she were home in her safe, cozy house.

A mile beyond the downtown, Robert turned again. The houses lining this street were some of the oldest in town and by far the most stately. Their lots were all larger than average, and the farther down the street one went, the farther apart were the houses. Finally, beyond the last streetlight, she saw Four Seasons. From a distance it appeared to be freshly painted and spanking new, but by the time they were into the drive, even the dim moonlight revealed its sagging gutters and the rough patch of paint that was peeling beneath a bow window. "It needs a lot of work," she said despondently.

"The house? It sure does. That's one of the things I dislike about old houses. As soon as you fix one thing, another breaks."

"It has charm," she said defensively. "Charm and character."

"I grew up in a house with character. I could hardly wait to get into a new one. Character usually means soft spots in the foundation and dry rot in the walls."

"It has no such thing."

"If I were you, I'd at least cut down that wisteria in back. So close to the house, its bound to be damaging that back wall."

"I'll do no such thing. I love that wisteria."

"Suit yourself. It's your house."

Lauren scowled at him, though she was sure it was wasted in the darkness. "The trouble with you is that you have no feel for tradition and grace in a house."

"Thanks a lot. That's probably why I'm stepping up as a partner in the company. They felt sorry for my lack of taste."

"Oh, you're a good architect. I didn't mean that. But there's more to a house than function and cost-saving design."

"Really? I never heard that before."

"Sarcasm doesn't become you, Robert."

He jerked the car to a stop, got out, then walked slowly around to her door. She knew he was composing himself. He seldom allowed his anger to show. When he opened her door,

Lauren offered him her hand so he could help her out of the car. After a moment's pause, he took it and helped her out. He really was such a gentleman when he tried to be, she thought.

She looked around the dark lawn. "I think I'll plant Kate Jessamines over there. Don't you think that would be nice?"

"What are they?" he asked in a disgruntled voice.

Lauren blinked. "What are gardenias?"

"I thought you said—"

"It doesn't matter. You don't like my house anyway."

"Do we have to argue about this?"

"Apparently we do."

"Lauren, I was the first in my entire family to get a formal education. I want to be somebody and do something. This house is like stepping backward for me."

"I see," she said frigidly.

They went up the front steps in silence, and Lauren fit her key into the lock. "We don't have to argue at all, Robert. I don't know why you're being so unpleasant."

"Me?"

She opened the door and breathed in the welcoming scent of her house—lemon oil, a faint mustiness of old floors and walls, a touch of cloves. "You'll come in, won't you? I could make some iced lemonade."

"Lemonade?"

"Coffee," she corrected. "I could make coffee."

"Are you feeling all right? You look awfully pale."

"Nonsense. I feel perfectly fine." She turned on the lights and smiled at the way the brightness glowed down the paneled hall. Crossing to the parlor she turned on those lights as well. "Robert?" she said when she realized he was still at the door. "Aren't you coming?"

He entered, but only a few steps. He was frowning up at the darkness in the top of the stairwell. "Do you really like being here alone at night? It's like spending the night in a museum."

"Don't start in on it again. I love it here." She turned back and entered the parlor. "Come to the kitchen and talk to me while I make coffee."

She passed through the rooms, leaving a trail of lights behind her. When she reached the kitchen, she paused and threw a glance at the well. Since the night of her panic attack, she hadn't felt easy around it. Averting her eyes, she went to the coffee pot.

"I wish I hadn't rushed into redecorating downstairs," she said as she spooned coffee into the pot. "I wish now that I had retained more of the house's original character."

"It has plenty left," Robert observed.

She ignored his derisive comment. "We never did get around to setting a wedding date."

"No," he said, almost as if he were speaking only to himself, "we didn't."

Abigail McDaniels

"I've always fancied being a June bride."
She laughed. "Of course that's not possible unless we wait another year. The month is almost
over."

Robert made no reply.

"Of course it wouldn't *have* to be an elaborate wedding. You know, with scads of brides-
maids and candles and me in a long white
gown. That's really more appropriate for a
young bride." Lauren's voice faltered. There
was that word again. Young.

She looked back at Robert. "Not that I'm
decrepit," she said with a quick laugh, "but
maybe a simpler ceremony would be better.
Just us and the preacher with Celia and Mark
as witnesses."

"I have my parents, too. And there's your
mother. Not to mention aunts and cousins who
would be bent out of shape if they weren't invited."

"That's true," she said absently. The house
was in one of its curious silences, as if it were
listening. She looked up at the ceiling as if she
could see through it and discern why the usual
sounds had stopped.

"Besides, I don't want to rush into it."

"Rush into it? We've dated seven years!"

"But we haven't been considering marriage
all that time, now have we? That's a fairly recent development."

She faced him squarely. "Are you saying you
don't want to marry me?"

"No, I'm not saying that. All I'm saying is

let's not do something we may regret." He looked so uncomfortable she almost felt sorry for him. "There's a lot we don't know about each other. I've never met your family, for instance, nor you mine."

"You aren't marrying my family, Robert. Besides, we aren't very close to one another."

"My family is. They live right here in Siddel Marsh."

Lauren took coffee cups out of the cabinet. "I've told you I'd like to meet them someday."

"How about tomorrow after work? I'll call Mom and tell her to expect us."

"I don't make good first impressions. You know I hate to meet people."

"That's nonsense. You meet people at the office all the time. She and Dad have been curious why you've refused to meet them."

"It's not that I'm refusing. I'm just nervous about meeting them. Okay?" Although the coffee hadn't quit perking, she poured each of them a cupful.

"All right, then I'll meet your mother first. Where does she live?"

"She's been sick," Lauren answered evasively. "It would be better not to upset her now." She tried never to introduce anyone to her mother. Somehow the conversation always seemed to drift to poor Aunt Mabel and to Lauren's junior year at college. "You can meet her after the wedding."

"She wouldn't want to be there?"

"She has chronic bad health. Mother doesn't

travel." She handed him the cup of weak coffee.

"Can't you see how odd that sounds?" Robert asked in exasperation. "I'm beginning to get the feeling you don't want me to meet your family. That you're ashamed of me or something."

"And I'm getting the impression that you want to examine my family tree before you'll agree to marry me," she snapped.

Robert put his cup on the countertop. "I ought to be going. Otherwise, we'll have another argument."

"Suit yourself. As usual."

They exchanged a mutual glare, and Lauren led him back to the front door by way of the drawing room and library.

Robert looked around at the lighted rooms. "The electric bill for this place must look like the national debt."

"That's something you don't have to worry about."

Robert looked down at her, a curious expression on his face, as if he had unanswered questions that he wasn't able to verbalize. "You're different," he finally repeated.

"You're imagining things." She opened the front door and waited for him to leave.

"No, I don't think I am. I just can't quite put my finger on it."

Lauren's headache was increasing again. "Good night, Robert."

Without replying, Robert kissed her on the

cheek and left. Lauren closed the door and leaned her aching head against it. Why had she ever decided to marry him in the first place? She wanted a man who could stand up to her and be head of the family, not someone who made excuses about meeting parents and such drivel as that.

Tears beaded her eyelashes and coursed down her cheeks. Couldn't Robert tell she only wanted what any woman would want—a man to protect her and take care of her, someone to buffer her against a world that was often too big and too harsh.

As these thoughts passed through her, Lauren's headache faded. She wanted, needed someone to look after her. She didn't like the idea of facing her future alone. She was a young woman and had years and years of loneliness ahead unless someone strong came along to care for her.

She heard Robert's car start up, and she turned the lock to secure the door. She didn't need him. He wasn't strong.

A sound came to her from the back of the house. Could she hear a droplet falling in the well from this distance? She had never noticed that before. Half-afraid of what she might hear, Lauren concentrated on the silence. After several minutes she decided she must have been mistaken. The well was at the far end of the house, and there were several closed doors in-between. All at once Lauren was tired, too tired to turn out the lights or unplug the coffee pot. She looked up as the grandfather clock on the landing sounded midnight.

Midnight? She and Robert had arrived at the restaurant at about 7:30, and they hadn't stayed there over an hour. Was it possible they had talked in the kitchen for hours? No, that couldn't be.

She looked down at her wristwatch and confirmed the time. Her eyes narrowed as she looked back at the grandfather clock. When had it started to run? Ever since she had moved in, it had stood silent and useless. And how on earth could it have started itself up at the proper time?

Slowly she went up the stairs and stopped in front of the clock. It was tall, much taller than herself, and made of polished cherry wood. The ivory face had gold hands and Roman numerals as well as a movement that showed the phase of the moon.

Cautiously she touched the glass case that protected the heavy pendulum which was swaying in pedantic arcs. When she lay her cheek on the glass she heard the solid ticking and almost inaudible whir of all its tiny wheels and cogs.

Lauren pulled back and straightened. She had heard of clocks that were wound too tight or whatever that suddenly started working again. Maybe that was all that had been wrong with this one. Some spring or lever had loosened over time and the clock had started ticking again. That it had started at the correct time was remarkable but wasn't any reason for her to feel afraid.

She looked back down at the brilliantly lit hall. Midnight. Where had the time gone?"

More puzzled than afraid, Lauren went upstairs to her room, leaving the hall and upper foyer bathed in light. All she wanted was to go to sleep.

As she undressed she thought about Robert. Looking back on it, she had been hard on him. She had always been assertive, but tonight she had lapsed over into aggressive. Still, Robert used to admire that in her. He said he liked a woman who knew what she wanted and wasn't afraid to go after it.

How absurd, she thought with a smile as she slipped on her nightgown. She wasn't assertive by nature; she only wanted someone to take care of her.

As she went to the bathroom to wash her face, she hummed a tune she had always loved about a gray bonnet with blue ribbons on it and a horse hitched to a shay. The song was about a golden wedding day. Would she ever have a golden anniversary? Or perhaps it meant the wedding day was golden with sunlight. For some reason she couldn't recall enough of the words to decide which it was.

She washed her face and studied her reflection in the mirror. As Robert had said, she did look pale, but she thought that was an improvement. She had never found dark, leathery skin to be attractive, at least not on a woman.

She wished her hair was longer so she could braid it before going to bed. It looked somehow unfinished, the way it only reached her jaw. She didn't care much for bobbed hair even if it was all the rage.

Turning off the bathroom light, Lauren stood for a minute looking at the opposite door that led to the blue room. Realizing how tired she was, she went back into the yellow room and pulled down the covers on her bed.

The sheets were cool against her body, and she lay there enjoying the luxury of her room. Above her the cornice boards surrounded the ceiling, and a fan drifted in lazy circles about the group of tulip-shaped light globes. The walls were more mustard than yellow in this light, and she told herself she really must decide on new wallpaper.

Far below her she thought she heard a noise. She sat up in bed and listened but heard nothing. As she tried to convince herself it was only her imagination, she heard it again. It was the sound of light switches being tripped. Someone was turning off the lights!

Before she could leap out of bed, first the stairwell, then the foyer went black. Lauren's heart thudded painfully in her throat. She tried to form words to demand who was there, but no sound came out.

Suddenly her bedroom lights winked out.

Lauren made a strangled gasp of fear and fumbled for the switch on her bedside lamp.

At last her fingers found the knob, and she twisted it on.

With frightened eyes she looked around the room. Her clothes lay draped across the chair just as she had left them. The closet door was still shut, and the bathroom door was still open.

Glancing into the empty bathroom, Lauren eased out of the bed and crossed to the closet. Taking a deep breath she yanked open the door. It was empty.

Lauren hastily shut it and turned back to the room. She was all alone. Beyond the open door yawned the blackness of the foyer and stairwell. She ran across the room and jumped into bed, afraid something might grab her by the ankle if she paused.

The house was silent. Outside a breeze ruffled the thick wisteria leaves around her window. On the landing the grandfather clock ticked softly.

The house is old, she told herself. The wiring is faulty.

But that didn't account for the clicking of the light switches or how the lights had gone off one at a time.

Lauren pulled the covers up to her chin. She wasn't sleepy anymore.

Chapter Six

Lauren wasn't having a good day. After lying awake most of the night before, she had fallen asleep just before dawn and had dreamed that someone just out of sight was calling her by the wrong name. The dream hadn't been all that unsettling, but it had awakened her. And the more alert she became, the more frightening was her recollection of the dream.

She arrived at work before Robert and managed to stay busy at her file cabinet until he went into his office. She was embarrassed over the argument she had had with Robert the night before and still wasn't sure where she stood with him.

When Celia came into the office Lauren gave

a start. "Hi. I didn't hear you come in. Shut the door, will you?"

Celia pushed the door closed and sat on one of the stuffed chairs usually reserved for Lauren's clients. "I noticed your car out front and thought I'd see if you're free for lunch today."

Lauren checked her desk calendar and nodded. "About noon? I'm to talk with a client at eleven, but I should be free by then."

"Perfect. Mr. Keane and Mr. Barlowe have court cases today, and since Mr. Horton is home sick I can take off."

"I wouldn't think lawyers would be all that busy in a town this size."

"It seems to hit in cycles. Right now everybody is suing everybody else."

"And the winners of those suits are using the settlements to add extra bedrooms and porches. This is the busiest we've been since I started to work here."

Celia curiously eyed her friend. "Are you feeling okay? You look tired."

Lauren turned away. "I didn't sleep well last night," she admitted. After a pause, she added, "I had an argument with Robert."

"You did?"

Lauren nodded. For some reason she was reluctant to tell Celia about the odd behavior of her lights. "I made the mistake of trying to pin him down to a wedding date and of assuming we would live at Four Seasons. He wasn't too happy about either subject."

"Well, for Pete's sake, you've dated for seven years. Everybody assumes you're going to be married."

"He proposed to me ages ago. I said yes. We weren't formally engaged with a ring and so on, and we haven't discussed it often, but I assumed we were engaged." She added a frown to the dark circles under her eyes. "I seem to be making a lot of wrong assumptions lately."

"Maybe he's just afraid of making such a permanent commitment. A lot of people are these days."

"He was actually upset at the idea of him moving into my house. Can you imagine that?"

Celia tactfully said nothing.

"I can't believe he would rather live in a new home with a bare lawn than in a lovely old Queen Anne like Four Seasons. I think his whole problem is that I didn't ask his permission and bow and scrape to do his bidding. Women's liberation hasn't made any inroads in Siddel Marsh."

"It wouldn't hurt to ask his opinion on a few things," Celia ventured.

"I can't stand manipulative women. If we want something, we should say so and not beat around the bush."

Celia studied her as if she were trying to decide how to respond.

"Maybe it's lack of exposure to the house. Robert hasn't been over a dozen times since I moved in."

"You seem more upset over him not wanting to live in the house than you are over him not wanting to set a wedding date."

Lauren ignored her. "I know what I can do. I'll have another party. What are you doing tomorrow night?"

"So soon?"

"It will be informal. I'll just have chips and dip."

"But it's a week night."

"So what? We're all adults and can stay up past nine o'clock."

Celia shrugged. "Okay with me. But I've never been to a party on a Tuesday night."

"Neither have I. This could be fun." Lauren opened the door to the outer office. "Party tomorrow night—my place." Everyone looked at her in surprise, but she seemed not to notice. "There. That's done."

"Shouldn't you have checked with Robert first?"

"What could he possibly have planned on a Tuesday night?" Lauren airily responded. She sat at her desk and leaned back in her chair. "All he needs is to get to know the place better. I'm sure he'll fall in love with it just like I did." She was thoughtful for a minute. "Maybe I'll have him over for supper tonight, too."

"Are you sure that's not overkill?"

"I can have that new casserole I told you about. And that burgundy he likes so well."

"Shouldn't you check with him before you get too far along with all this?"

"Do you suppose Susan will come? I'm positive she heard the invitation. I always feel uneasy with her around."

"You should have thought of that before you announced it to everyone in the office."

"Maybe she won't come. Mr. Combe was out there, too, and you *know* he won't come over to my house."

"Your boss is here?" Celia hastily rose to her feet. "I had no idea it was so late. I have to be running."

Lauren absently nodded.

"Should I bring anything tomorrow?"

"Just whatever you want to drink. I'm keeping it simple. And Mark is invited."

"Great. See you at noon." Celia waved and slipped out.

Lauren pushed aside the drawings she was supposed to be working on and began sketching the green bedroom of her house. There was no time to start redecorating it before the party, of course, but she had decided in the night that it would make a better nursery than the yellow room. Like the red room, it was slightly smaller than the other two bedrooms and had a connecting bath. And, as with all the bedrooms, it not only opened onto the central foyer, but to the upper veranda on the outside as well. With so many doors and windows it was a challenge to decorate.

Hours later she looked up in surprise as Susan knocked on the door. "The Flournoys are here already?"

Susan nodded as she held the door for the older couple.

Lauren pulled out the lap drawer of her desk and slipped the bedroom drawings out of sight. Guiltily, she shuffled the Flournoys's house drawings over her desk top. Where had the morning gone? She hadn't touched her work for the day. "Have a seat, please," she said, casting a professional smile at the couple. "Here are the drawings I've been working on for your summer house."

Mr. Flournoy carefully inspected one of them. "It looks just the way it did the last time we were here."

"Oh, no, sir. See? I've moved the bath to this corner and added these new cabinets in the kitchen."

The couple exchanged a glance at one another. "Weren't those changes made the last time?" Mrs. Flournoy asked. "They look familiar to me. And where's the sun deck with the built-in planters we asked for? Is the picture of the outside in here?" She shuffled the top sketch aside revealing a half-completed exterior view.

"Those aren't finished yet." Lauren tried to smile reassuringly.

"Still? They weren't finished last time, either." Mr. Flournoy cocked his head to one side as if he was becoming quite suspicious.

A dull headache was settling behind Lauren's eyes, and she rubbed her forehead to ease it. "I . . . I had them ready for you, but I acci-

111

dentally dropped them in the rain." She knew she wasn't lying well; she never had.

"Rain?"

"Last week. It rained last week." She tried to remember if the couple had been in before or after the rain storm, but the memory eluded her. "Look, I apologize. I really do. I promise I'll have everything ready to show you by our next meeting."

"You said that last time."

"I'm sorry, Mr. Flournoy. That's all I can say."

With a frown, Mrs. Flournoy was examining the sketch Lauren had pushed aside. "What's this mark mean?"

Lauren leaned nearer and blinked. After a moment she said, "That's the way we indicate a well." Her headache was increasing.

"Why would we want a well in our kitchen?" the woman asked. "We aren't building *that* far out in the country."

"I know. I don't recall why I put it there." She didn't remember drawing it there at all. "Of course you don't want a well in the kitchen."

"We want regular plumbing. You understand that, don't you? Regular plumbing!"

"Of course you do. Remember the nice bathroom we discussed with the Jacuzzi tub?"

The Flournoys looked a bit more reassured.

"Don't worry. This will be a lovely summer place. I'll tell you what. How about coming by again on Wednesday, and I'll have the finished plans by then."

"Wednesday? Day after tomorrow?"

Lauren nodded. She would have to put aside some of her other projects, but she didn't want to lose this assignment. The Flournoys were influential and might send her a number of other retirement-aged couples if she kept them pleased.

"All right. We'll be back on Wednesday," Mr. Flournoy said.

Lauren smiled with relief and stood until they left her office. Slowly she sat down again and rubbed her aching head. How had she managed to forget to work on their house? And why on earth had she drawn a well in their modern kitchen?

Lauren pushed the Flournoys' drawings aside and retrieved the sketch of her green bedroom. Without hesitation, she resumed drawing in the new lintels and cornice boards and jotted down notes concerning colors and fabrics.

Lauren balanced the bag of groceries on her hip as she struggled with the key to her kitchen door. This door had been difficult to unlock ever since she had moved in, and now it seemed to have given it up altogether. In exasperation she jiggled the knob and cursed herself for not updating the door locks. At the time, it had seemed romantic to use skeleton keys on all the doors.

Finally she gave up and circled the veranda to the parlor door, which opened with relative ease. As she kicked it shut, she noticed the ferns and ivy plants by the parlor windows were in dire need of water. She had been too busy lately to pay them any attention.

"Great," she muttered as she carried the heavy bag through to the kitchen. When ferns weren't watered properly, they tended to scatter leaves everywhere, and hers had been no exception.

She put the sack on the kitchen counter and flexed her tired arms. The sacker at the grocery store, being new to the job, had put all her groceries in one sack when he should have used two. And because the garage originally had been a carriage house and stable, it was quite a distance from the house. That was one of the inconveniences of living in an older house, she decided. People accustomed to servants hadn't thought of step-saving conveniences.

She put away all but the ingredients she would need for the casserole. A glance at the clock told her she was already pressed for time. Robert hadn't been exactly thrilled over her last-minute dinner invitation or over the party on a Tuesday night, but he had agreed to come to both.

Lauren turned on the oven and reminded herself again to water her house plants as she fished the new casserole recipe out of her recipe box and began dinner preparations.

Cooking took longer than she had expected.

What had sounded simple on paper involved more steps than was apparent. Outside she heard the dull. rumble of thunder roll across the lake. A glance out the window showed the sky was darkening beneath scudding clouds. Again the weather forecast had been wrong. Feeling a bit jittery, she glanced at the clock. It was already after 6:30. The newspaper would probably be in the yard by now. Thunder purred over the lake. There was no time to bring the paper in now.

Lauren hurried upstairs and turned on the newly installed shower before undressing. Robert was always punctual, and he might be upset if she kept him waiting. As she wadded her clothes into the wicker hamper, she wondered if she should give him a key. That might help her convince him to think of the house as his own, but she was reluctant to pursue the thought. In a way she preferred to have the house all to herself.

She let the water sluice her clean, then vigorously towel-dried her hair. She had read that ultra-clean hair went a long way toward impressing a man. It sounded like something from a teen magazine, but it also held a ring of truth. As she pulled the brush through it and blew it dry with her hair dryer, she considered letting it grow out, even though she was already wearing it longer than she ever had in her life. Lately she had found herself wanting to wear it in a classic chignon or maybe a Gibson girl style. She critically studied her face in the steamy mirror. She had features that would be attractive in that style.

She put on only a bare minimum of makeup—just a touch of brown eye shadow and mascara the color of her own lashes—not because she was in a hurry, but because in recent weeks she had pulled away from more formal makeup. There was time for all that when she was older and would need the artifice.

Lauren blinked and studied her reflection more closely. She should have taken the time to apply makeup base to conceal the tiny lines at the corners of her eyes and mouth. Slowly she reached up and touched her cheek, as if it were the face of a stranger. Was she getting old? Already?

Self-consciously, she pulled herself away from the mirror and ran to dress, the bedside clock reminding her she had only ten minutes. Quickly, she took one of her new dresses from the closet and drew it on over her head. She had gone all the way to Shreveport for it, but it had been worth the trip. The dress was the color of candlelight on cream and had a frothy jabot and pearl buttons. The skirt was full and longer than the ones she usually wore. At the neck she fastened a rose-hued cameo she had found in an antique shop.

Again she studied herself in the mirror. The dress had exactly the right effect. If only her hair were long enough to sweep up into a bun with loose tendrils about her face. As she was considering teasing it into a bouffant to resemble a bun, the doorbell rang.

Shoving her feet into her shoes, Lauren glanced around her bedroom. If all went well they would finish the evening here, and she wanted it to look perfect. She turned off the light and hurried downstairs.

As she reached the lower hall she gave it a quick inspection. It was neat and clean. The mirror bore no smudges, and the table beneath the newspaper gleamed with polish. Newspaper?

Lauren went to the table and picked up the paper. It lay exactly where she would have put it if she had brought it in, but she hadn't. There hadn't been time to go out to the front yard and get it. As she stared at it, her mind rejected all the possible explanations for its appearance there on the table.

Again the bell rang, and Lauren looked up, her eyes startled. Quickly she went to the door and opened it. "Robert. Come in." Of course! That would explain it. Robert had brought in the paper. So why was it inside and Robert still on the porch? "Thanks for bringing in my paper. My goodness, but it's starting to rain hard. Did you get very wet?"

Robert shook his head. "Not very wet. Is that a new dress?"

Lauren smiled radiantly and turned around for him to admire it. "Yes. Do you like it?"

"It's nice. It matches the house."

She wasn't too sure whether he had intended

that as a compliment, knowing how he felt about Four Seasons. "Supper will be ready by now. I hope you're hungry. I'm trying a new casserole."

"It smells good."

Lauren returned the newspaper to the hall table and led Robert into the dining room. "Just have a seat while I bring it in."

"In here? Why so formal?" he asked with a laugh. "I'm used to eating in a kitchen. Remember?"

"I know we always have before, but now that I have a dining room, we may as well use it." She handed him a small box of matches. "Will you light the candles?"

"Sure."

She went into the kitchen and opened the oven. The casserole smelled even better than she had hoped it would. Now that she had her own house, she decided she would do more cooking—and more entertaining, too. The house had been designed for parties and could easily be arranged for either intimate gatherings or formal affairs.

Robert was lighting the last candle in the spreading candelabra when Lauren returned and set the steaming casserole on the silver trivet. "Want me to help bring in the food?" he offered.

"This is it except for the bread. Just have a seat here." She nodded toward the chair at the head of the table.

The bread was already on the silver serving

dish. Lauren covered it with a white linen napkin and smiled. Buying the silver had put a considerable dent in her bank account, but it was worth it.

Robert was sitting at the end of the table, his back to the kitchen door. Lauren paused to smile again at the back of his head. He looked so proper there. She nudged the light off with her elbow. Robert looked back at her in surprise.

"Don't you think it's a bit dark with the lights off?" he asked.

"Of course not. That's why I had you light the candles." She put the bread on the table and looked around. With only the bread and casserole on the long table, the white linen cloth looked bare. "Next time I must prepare more food," she said absently.

"Looks great." Robert gave her an encouraging grin. "I'm starved."

Lauren passed her plate to him to be served as the casserole was too hot to pass. She should have invited more of their friends to fill the big table, but the two of them had always been enough for each other. "Thank you . . . Robert," she said as she took back her plate. For a second she had almost called him by the wrong name. Confusion touched her. He was the only man she had dated for years. What name could she possibly have confused with his?

When Robert had helped his own plate, Lauren lifted her fork. He seemed so suited to the room with his dark hair and broad shoulders.

119

She had never noticed before that he was so well-built. She made a mental note not to take him so much for granted.

"Are these new plates?" he asked.

"Yes. Do you like them?"

"Sure. I just didn't know you needed any new ones."

"My everyday china was too informal for the dining room. I plan to do more entertaining. It's a service for twelve."

"Twelve?"

"I just couldn't pass them up." She lifted the fork to her mouth and tasted the casserole. A frown touched her forehead. Something wasn't right about this.

Robert also tasted it. His eyes met hers. He tried to smile.

Lauren lay down her fork and said, "Are you playing tricks on me, Robert?"

"I don't know what you're talking about."

"First the newspaper and now this. You salted the casserole."

"I don't know what—"

"While I was in the kitchen, you deliberately put too much salt in our food." She stared at him accusingly.

"I did no such thing. I admit it's pretty salty, but that's not my fault. You must have measured out the wrong amount when you were cooking it."

"That's impossible. I can certainly follow a simple recipe."

He valiantly took another bite. "It's not that bad."

"It certainly is. I can't eat food that's so salty." She glared at him.

"Don't look at me that way. You know I'm not into practical jokes."

Lauren turned her head. Robert was right, he rarely joked at all. She tried another bite of food and only swallowed it with difficulty. She had never liked salty food, and Robert knew it.

"Look," he said, covering her hand with his own, "why don't we go out for dinner?"

"I worked for an hour or more on this." She felt perilously close to tears.

"I know you must have, but sometimes new recipes simply don't turn out the way you think they will." He smiled. "I know you don't cook often and are disappointed at the way this turned out."

"Not cook often?"

"Maybe there was a typo in the recipe."

He looked so sincere, she wanted to believe him. How odd, though, that he would accuse her of not cooking very often. Lauren loved to entertain. That was one reason she was so fond of this house. Her thoughts went back to the newspaper. "Robert, do you have a key to this house?"

"A key? No, of course not."

She tried to remember if she had had to turn the lock to let him in. Maybe the door hadn't been locked, and he had opened it, put the paper on the table and stepped back out again. It was possible.

"Do you want to go out?" he asked again.

"No, no, don't be silly. I'll make us a salad." She stood up and reached for her pot holders on the side table.

Robert opened the door for her and, after blowing out the candles, followed her into the kitchen. The smell of burnt candlewicks drifted in with him.

"You could have waited in the dining room," she said. "It won't take me long to put together a salad."

"I don't mind helping."

"I think I can be trusted to make a simple salad," she stiffly retorted.

He sighed and turned his eyes to the ceiling as he so often did when he was becoming exasperated. "I didn't mean that."

Lauren dumped the casserole into the wastebasket and put the dish in the sink. Why had Robert ruined it? If he had thought such a prank would be funny, he was developing a very peculiar sense of humor. Lauren had always detested practical jokes. She opened her recipe box and reread the recipe. It didn't call for any salt at all.

Robert had taken a head of lettuce from her refrigerator and was searching for salad bowls. She let him look. "I don't have any of the salad dressing you like."

"That's okay. Bottled is fine."

"I mean I only have Thousand Island. What did you think I meant?"

He found the bowls and took out two. "I like the buttermilk kind that comes in those packets."

"Since when?" She turned and stared at him.

He shrugged. "I guess I had it somewhere and liked it."

She frowned. Had some other woman prepared it for him? Lately the house had kept her so busy, she hadn't seen Robert as often as before. She took a tomato from the refrigerator and put it on the chopping block. Her fingers closed around the handle of a large knife, and as she picked it up, the blade reflected the bright kitchen light. For a minute the sparkle fascinated her. Slowly she drew the sharp blade through the flesh of the tomato. Red juice ran over her fingers.

"Do you have any boiled eggs?"

Lauren looked up in surprise.

"Boiled eggs," Robert repeated. "I thought you liked eggs in your salad."

"Oh, I do. There should be some in the bowl on the shelf beside the milk." She looked at the small pieces of tomato and swallowed nervously. She didn't remember dicing it.

"I found them," Robert said cheerfully.

Lauren put the tomatoes in the bowls and rinsed the cutting board and knife. Outside the windows, night had closed about the house. Rain still pattered on the roof, but the torrents

123

had slackened into a steady downpour. Lightning flashed, momentarily revealing the rough surface of the lake, then snuffing it from view. Uneasily Lauren turned away but had to glance back out as thunder rumbled. "It's so dark out here in the country," she murmured.

"Siddel Marsh is a far cry from city life. Do you ever miss it?"

"No." She put her back toward the window and got silverware out of the drawer.

"Don't you get lonesome here?" Robert asked.

"Lonesome?"

"This house is so big for one person. I'm surprised you want to live here."

"I won't always live here alone. Eventually you'll be here, too. Then in time there will be children." She poured them each a glass of iced tea.

Robert looked uncomfortable. "I'd be upset if I thought you bought this house only because you assumed . . . well, something we haven't really decided."

She laughed a bit too gaily. "We've discussed marriage. You know we have. And naturally that means children."

"Let's not get into that again." He found the bottle of salad dressing he had been looking for and put it on the table.

"You want to eat in here? In the kitchen?"

"I'd prefer it."

She put the glasses of tea on the table and sat in one of the chairs as if she felt extremely awkward doing so. "Very well, Robert."

Again lightning illuminated the lake's choppy surface. It looked like mottled silver, and Lauren was fascinated by it. The water would feel cool, almost cold, if she were to wade out in it. "Do you like to swim?" she asked as he sat across from her.

"Not much. You know that."

"I guess I forgot." She tasted her salad. At least it wasn't salty. "I hadn't planned to eat in here."

Robert didn't answer.

"I wanted tonight to be special." She reached out and took his hand. "We haven't been as close lately as I'd like for us to be. It's my fault, really. I've been so busy."

"I understand." He refused to meet her eyes.

"What have you been doing with yourself while I was busy?"

Robert looked up. "What do you mean by that?"

Lauren found she wasn't anxious to pursue the topic. "It's warm in here. Do you think the storm knocked out my new air-conditioning unit?"

"It seems unlikely that it would go off when the lights haven't."

"But it's quite warm in here. Don't you think it's warm?"

Robert put down his fork and went over to the thermostat that was located just inside the drawing room door. "Here's the problem.

You've turned the temperature setting as high as it goes."

"I couldn't have." Lauren came to look at the needle. "It's on the proper setting."

"It is now. I just changed it." He glanced up at the vent. "See? It's already starting to blow cool air."

Lauren glowered at him. Had it been turned to a higher setting, or was Robert only telling her that? "How did you know where the thermostat had been installed?"

"I'm an architect. Remember? The thermostat is always located near the return air grille."

"Or maybe you changed the setting when you brought in the newspaper." She watched him closely to see his reaction.

"What are you talking about?"

"I'm not angry that you were in the house. I only want you to admit it."

Robert handed her his napkin. "I think I should go."

"Go?"

"For some reason you seem determined to provoke an argument. Since I don't want to fight with you, I think it would be best if I left."

"I think so, too," she frostily replied.

She stalked ahead of him to the front door and threw it open. The sound of rain rushed in. "Good night, Robert." She drew herself up as tall as possible.

He seemed about to say something but shook his head and went out into the storm.

Lauren shut the door more firmly than was necessary and gave the dead bolt a hard twist. This time the door was locked for sure.

She went back to the kitchen and sat down to finish her salad, but she couldn't eat with Robert's half-filled salad bowl, a symbol of the failed evening, next to hers.

As she started to remove his bowl, the lightning flashed again, and Lauren thought she saw the figure of a man on her back porch. She held her breath, staring at the darkened window until the next flash showed her she must have seen the thick trunk of the wisteria and mistaken it for a man. For a minute there she had thought Robert had circled around back for another of his pranks. The door lock was broken, however, and until she had a locksmith out, no one was going in or out that way.

Deciding she could ignore Robert's uneaten salad, Lauren finished eating and washed the dishes. She was reluctant to watch television during such a storm for fear of damage to the set, but she didn't feel like reading.

She filled a pitcher with water and went to take care of her neglected house plants. She pushed aside the leaves of the fern and poured a generous amount of water into the pot. At once it overflowed. Lauren caught as much of the excess water as was possible in the pitcher and then got a towel to sop up the spill that shouldn't have happened. Cautiously she felt the soil in the pot of ivy beside the fern and found it was moist. So were all the others.

Lauren backed to the sideboard and put the pitcher on a trivet. Her hands were trembling so hard some of the water sloshed out onto the oak top. She wiped it up.

Although she had always heard it was dangerous to use the telephone in an electrical storm, she went to it and dialed Celia's number.

"Celia? Can you talk a minute?" Lauren tried to keep the fear out of her voice.

"I thought Robert was coming over tonight."

Lauren felt better after hearing her friend's calm tones. "He has already left." Her eyes went back to the pot plants. "I know this sounds really silly, but could you come over?"

"Now? In this storm? I already have on my nightgown. Is something the matter?"

"No, no." Lauren forced herself to laugh. "I told you it's silly. Robert has played some tricks on me, and that, combined with the storm, has made me uneasy. Of course you shouldn't come over. I'm being a big baby."

"Robert is playing tricks? The same Robert I know?"

"Unbelievable, isn't it? Maybe he's developing a sense of humor—of sorts."

"What kind of tricks?"

Again Lauren forced herself to laugh. "He seems to have been in my house while I was upstairs taking a shower. He brought in the newspaper, watered the plants and readjusted the air-conditioning thermostat."

"Those don't sound amusing."

"But he denied doing them. When I came downstairs, he was on the porch, ringing the doorbell as if he had just arrived."

"That's odd. Are you sure he did those things?"

"Well, who else could have?" Lauren snapped, then immediately regretted her temper outburst. "I'm sorry. I didn't mean to bark at you. It's just eerie to find all these things changed and not be able to explain them. I'm sure Robert must have done them, though. Who else could have?"

Celia paused. "I don't suppose you could have done them and forgotten that you had?"

"Impossible!"

"Okay, okay. Don't get upset."

Lauren slipped off her shoes and drew her feet up under her body. "There's only one other explanation. Do you suppose it's possible someone else has a key to this place?" She gripped the receiver and hoped Celia would reassure her this was unlikely and laugh away her fears.

"You mean some stranger?"

"I didn't change the locks when I moved in. There's a dead bolt on the front door, but all the others work with skeleton keys. Someone could have a copy, couldn't he?"

"I guess it's possible," Celia admitted, "but it's awfully unlikely. I mean, what stranger would bring in the paper and water plants? Or care if your house is a particular temperature?"

Lauren relaxed a bit. "That doesn't make sense, does it? I guess the storm has me spooked."

"I would be nervous, too, alone in that big old house. Have you ever considered taking in boarders?"

"You can't be serious."

"Why not? It would give you some daily company."

"I don't want strangers coming and going in my house. It's out of the question."

"Okay. I only thought I'd mention it."

Lauren shifted the phone receiver to her other ear. "I don't suppose you came over and did those things for me?"

"Me? You think I'd come into your house without permission? Lauren!"

"I had to ask. I'm sorry. Okay?" She could hear how upset Celia was at the very idea. "It had to have been Robert."

"I suppose." Celia still sounded miffed.

"I have a hard time picturing him playing practical jokes, though. Not Robert."

"Well, I only know it wasn't me."

"I guess I had better get off the phone. I'm sorry I upset you."

"That's okay. I'm edgy, too."

Lauren said good-bye and hung up. For several minutes she sat hugging her legs beneath her and staring at the group of potted plants.

Thunder rattled the windows, and Lauren hastily stood up. Without blinds or curtains on any of the downstairs windows, she knew she would be clearly visible to anyone looking through the windows into the brightly lit interior.

But despite her concern about being watched, she left on the lights because she was afraid to go up in the dark. Although she knew the doors were locked, she checked them again, then dashed up the stairs.

As her room was pitch black, she stopped at the doorway and reached in for the light switch. As she groped about, her fingers encountered and passed through something cool and too thick to be air. Stifling a scream, Lauren jabbed at the light switch, sending brilliance into every corner of the room.

No one was there.

Chapter Seven

On the way to the locksmith, Lauren bought half a dozen flashlights with extra batteries for each. She had never been afraid of the dark, but the odd electrical quirks of her house were beginning to make her more than a little uneasy. The night before as she was going to bed the lights had pulled their vanishing act again. Logically she knew it was because the wiring was most probably almost as old as the house, but she disliked being plunged into total darkness.

Most of her morning had been spent in making lists of things she would need for the party that evening. Her work was suffering, but Lauren found she didn't really care. In the long run, parties such as this could be a better investment in her career than her ability to turn out a blueprint. Robert would soon be a full partner at Newton and Combe, and he would be expected to entertain important clients. Lauren knew she was the obvious choice to serve as his hostess. Once they were married, she would probably quit work anyway. Her time would be spent with the children and in giving intimate teas for all the right people.

She paused before the shop window of Siddel Marsh's best dress shop, but only to look. Lauren had always maintained that a woman who was a native of the town and regularly shopped there could be spotted at a distance by the polyester fabrics of her clothing. The store window again bore out her theory—not a natural-fibered dress among the lot.

She shifted the bag of flashlights to her other arm. They hadn't seemed heavy in the store, but she was tired of carrying them. Whatever had happened, she mused, to the days when ladies were not expected to carry their own parcels on the street? After stopping by the locksmith's shop and giving him her address, she headed home.

On her way, Lauren followed an impulse and detoured to the antique store a few blocks from the center of town. For a minute she sat in her car, debating whether or not to go inside. This was almost certainly the place where Susan Redlow had bought the Ouija board, and for that reason Lauren had previously avoided the place. But now here she was outside the store, unsure as to what had prompted her to come. Soon, the car became uncomfortably warm from the heat of the day, and Lauren decided it wouldn't hurt to go inside and look around.

A silver bell attached to the top of the door tinkled as she entered the store. The proprietor, a bald man with thick eyeglasses, nodded to her and smiled before going back to reading his newspaper. Lauren nodded in a detached way that signified she was friendly but not in the mood for conversation. This technique had worked for her in cities, and although she had never found it to be effective in Siddel Marsh, she always tried it in the hopes that someone, somewhere, would understand and let her shop undisturbed.

"Got some new things in," the man said as he glanced through the sports section. "In the back room. Just unpacked them."

"Thank you," Lauren dispassionately responded. She wasn't interested in a new shipment. She was wondering if any of the antiques on display were part of the Padgett estate. It stood to reason some might be since the Ouija board evidently had been.

Most of the furniture was made of oak, heavy and scaled to rooms of a size that had not been built in the last three or four decades. Many of the wardrobes and sideboards couldn't even fit into a modern room with their typically low ceilings, but even the tallest of them could be easily accommodated by the 12-foot-high ceilings of Four Seasons. Lauren wanted to eventually sell all her modern furniture and buy antiques that were proportionately sized for her house. She shuddered to think what Robert's chrome and glass furniture would look like in her house. The idea was so ludicrous, it made her smile.

Along the walls of the shop and scattered about on the tops of the furniture were unusual pieces of glassware and oil-burning lamps, some of which had been converted to electricity. She touched the rim of a flow-blue dinner plate and marveled at the outrageously high price tag. Did the owner actually sell anything at these prices? She decided most of his clients must be tourists who were passing through or collectors looking for a unique piece.

The next room was devoted to the more primitive pieces of furniture and kitchen odds and ends. These didn't interest her. Pine would look out of place in Four Season's elegant rooms.

The back room housed his antique quilts and linens and needlework. Lauren strolled through the quilts, looking for one with just the right colors for her bedroom. Instead she found one with a blue and white snowflake design that would be perfect for the sleigh bed in the blue room. This price, too, was staggering, but she decided to buy it anyway. It really made more sense to redecorate the master bedroom than it did the one that would soon be a guest room.

On the back wall were several nightgowns

and some blouses that caught her attention. Out of curiosity she went closer. None of the gowns were her size, but two of the blouses looked as if they had been made for her. She put down the quilt and held one of the blouses up to her. She had never seen more lovely needlework. All the rows of pleats and laces were sewn by hand with tiny stitches surpassing any machine work. One blouse was white, the other a pale yellow. Lauren knew she had to have them both.

As she hurried home, hoping she hadn't missed the locksmith's visit, she pondered the notion of hiring a servant. The small room in the attic was well-suited, and it would be more convenient for her if she didn't have to rush about to accommodate workmen's schedules.

After putting away the flashlights and hanging her blouses in the closet, she took the blue quilt into the adjoining room and spread it over the bed. It was exactly the right size to tuck in on each side and would serve well as a coverlet. She was amazed to see how much it brightened the room. There seemed to be less work needed on the Winter room than she had first assumed.

A knock on the door sent Lauren hurrying downstairs. The locksmith stood on her front porch. Lauren considered motioning for him to go to the side door, but decided against it. If he left she would never be able to get that back door repaired.

"Locksmith," he said unnecessarily. "Problems?"

Even after all the years she had been here, she still found the abbreviated manner of speech used by the locals to be a thing of curiosity. "Yes, my back door lock is broken."

The man grinned. "I'll bet I can fix it."

She suppressed a sigh. Not only did workmen these days come to the front door, but they seemed to expect the mistress of the house to engage in verbal banter. She led him through the house to the kitchen.

"Wow! Big place. Ever get lost?" he asked with another grin.

"Frequently." She pointed at the back door. "That's the one."

With a great show of expertise the man opened his metal tool box and knelt beside the door.

Lauren turned away to make a list of all the places to put flashlights.

"What seems to be wrong with it?" he asked.

"It doesn't work." She was trying to keep her tone civil, but she really resented his attitude.

"Seems to work now."

She turned to see the door swing open. "The key wouldn't turn before."

The man shrugged. "These old skeleton keys are tricky."

She glared at him. "I'm telling you it was broken."

"Come try it now."

Lauren shut the door and turned the key. The lock clicked easily into place. She tried it from the opposite side with the same results. "I don't understand."

"Looks to me like your husband was working on it. See here where the metal is shiny? Somebody must have taken it apart, oiled it and put it back together."

A sour taste that Lauren recognized as fear rose in her mouth. "Are you sure?"

"As sure as I can be. Why not ask him when he comes home tonight? I'll bet he did it to save you a repair bill."

Lauren pulled her eyes away from the lock. "Thank you for coming out. What do I owe you?"

"Nothing at all. I didn't do a thing." He grinned again. "Around here we don't charge an arm and a leg like they do in a city."

She led him back through the house and carefully locked the door behind him. Someone had worked on the lock. That had to mean someone had been in her house. Anyone who was capable of repairing the lock could likely come and go as he pleased. She drew the lace curtains aside and suspiciously watched the locksmith as he drove away. He could have done it. He had the tools and the expertise.

Slowly she let the curtain fall back into place. But if the locksmith was breaking into her house, he wouldn't have been so foolish as to point out to her that the lock had been tampered with. He would have merely pretended to fix it and leave again.

She raised her eyes and looked up the shadowy stairwell. Was someone in the house even now?

As silently as possible she circled through all the downstairs rooms, then the upstairs bedrooms. Nothing. After a long pause to gather her courage, she went up the narrow stairs to the attic. Yellow-gray light filtered through the dusty windows, and her heart hammered as she crept through the adjoining rooms, finally pushing open the door to the servant's room. Again nothing. The house was empty.

With a nervous glance over her shoulder, Lauren went back down to her bedroom. Sitting on the side of her bed, she tried to think. There could easily be someone else in the house and her not find him. The rooms all interconnected with each other as well as with a central hall, and a clever person could hide by moving from one room to the next, either ahead or behind her. The idea wasn't reassuring.

Far below she heard the sound of the telephone. Lauren ran down to answer it and grabbed it up on the fifth ring. "Hello?"

"Lauren, where the hell are you?"

"Obviously I'm at home, Robert."

"Why aren't you at work?" He sounded angry.

"I had to take the afternoon off. I have a dozen things I need to do."

"Must I remind you that you also have a job?

What are you doing that's so important that you can walk out in the middle of the day?"

"Please don't use that tone of voice on me, Robert. I'm not a servant, you know." There was a long pause. Lauren used it to get her temper under control. "Wait until you see what I bought." She knew he would love the snowflake quilt as much as she did.

"You've been shopping?" Robert sounded as if his temper was still heating up rather than cooling down.

"I see you're in no mood to hear about it now. I'll show it to you later." The dark blue in the quilt matched the blue of his eyes. Absently, Lauren rubbed her forehead. Or were Robert's eyes brown? "You won't be late tonight, will you?"

"Are you still determined to have a party tonight?"

"Of course. I've already invited everyone. You know that." She frowned. "You *are* coming, aren't you?" '

"I suppose. Yes, I'll be there. But Lauren, don't leave work again without permission. I've had the devil of a time covering up for you."

She smiled. "That's sweet of you, Robert, but really it's not necessary."

Again there was silence from his end.

"Was there anything else?" she prompted. "I have so much to do."

"I guess not."

"In that case, I'll see you tonight." She hung

up and smiled down at the receiver. Robert could be so sweet at times. That was true love, for him to take time out of his work day to phone her.

She went upstairs and began distributing the flashlights.

Celia was the first to arrive with Mark. Lauren ushered them in.

"Is that a new blouse?" Celia asked, sounding somewhat doubtful.

"Yes. Don't you love it?" Lauren had decided to wear the white one with her plain, floor-length black skirt. She had teased her hair into a fluffy shape and twisted a top-knot of her hair into a semblance of a bun.

Celia touched a frayed place on the blouse's cuff. "Where did you find this? And what have you done to your hair?"

Lauren beamed at her. She knew she looked especially good tonight. "It's a new place I found. I may start buying all my clothes there."

Celia made no comment, but she wondered what Lauren saw in the blouse. It was so old it seemed too fragile to wear, and with that black skirt it looked like a costume from a prairie days festival. She wasn't at all sure what to make of Lauren's new hair style, but it seemed to be geared to the rest of the costume.

"Just go in and make yourselves at home," Lauren was saying. "I think I hear another guest arriving."

Celia and Mark followed Lauren's gesture toward the drawing room, where they found a bowl of chips and another bowl of dip on the game table.

"Is this supposed to be a costume party?" Mark whispered, after glancing over his shoulder to be sure he was out of Lauren's earshot.

"Nostalgia is very big these days," Celia said loyally. She looked around the room. A fine layer of dust covered the table as well as the mantel. She knew Lauren was usually an immaculate housekeeper, and she hoped the dust wouldn't embarrass her. As she was debating whether she should run a cloth over the table and mantel before anyone else arrived, she heard voices in the hall. There was no time now.

Susan Redlow came into the room, followed closely by Robert. Lauren was behind them. "Are you positive Mr. Newton and Mr. Combe aren't coming?" she was asking Robert.

"You've got to be kidding. On a Tuesday? Besides, Mr. Combe is already upset with you over this afternoon."

"Perhaps if I telephone them and speak to their wives," Lauren suggested.

"Are you trying to get yourself fired?"

Celia looked from one to the other. "Is there some problem?"

"Not really." Robert's voice was tinged with sarcasm. "Lauren just decided to skip work today."

Lauren gave Celia a smile as if she expected

her friend to share in her amusement at what men thought was important. "You're making a mountain out of a molehill, Robert. Really!"

Celia went to stand by the wing-backed chair where Mark was sitting. Something was wrong here, but she couldn't quite put her finger on it. "Do you want me to help you with drinks?"

"If you'd like. Coffee, anyone? Sherry?"

"Sherry?" Robert questioned with ill-humor. "I'll take a Scotch."

Lauren blinked as if she were surprised, but she took it in stride. "What about the rest of you?"

"Coffee," Susan murmured in her timid, apologetic voice.

"Scotch sounds great to me," Mark said.

Celia followed Lauren into the kitchen where a coffee pot was bubbling away. "The Scotch is in the sideboard," Lauren said. "If you'd rather, I'll get it."

"I can manage."

Celia found glasses in the massive sideboard and poured two drinks. Concerned for her friend, she went back to talk with her in private. "Lauren, are you feeling all right?"

"Perfectly." Lauren looked at her in surprise. "Why do you ask that?"

"No reason."

Lauren put the coffee cups on a silver tray. "Do you use cream or sugar?"

"Cream, just like always." Celia touched the gleaming side of a silver sugar bowl. "Isn't this new? I didn't know you had a silver service."

"I bought it last week. Now that I'll be entertaining more often, I need it."

"It must have cost a bundle."

"It wasn't cheap," Lauren agreed with one of her familiar grins.

Celia relaxed somewhat. "What's this about you not going to work this afternoon?"

Lauren shrugged as she put the silver cream pitcher on the tray. "I had a lot of things I needed to do."

Celia's eyes followed Lauren's movements. "Real cream? Not a substitute? I'm impressed."

Lauren winked at her. "Let's hope Robert is." She took the drinks from Celia and placed them on the tray, then swept back into the drawing room.

As Lauren put the tray on the table, Celia handed the Scotch to the men. She could tell from the displeased look on Robert's face that he, too, had noticed the dusty table. Celia wished she had come over earlier to help Lauren get ready for the party, but she hadn't expected it to be anything but informal. Everyone but Lauren was wearing casual clothes.

Celia sat in the chair opposite Mark but couldn't get comfortable. Feeling behind the seat cushion, Celia discovered what was poking her and pulled out Lauren's hairbrush.

"Where did you get that?" Lauren exclaimed.

"It was behind the cushion. Have you been searching for it?"

Lauren took it and glanced up as if to look upstairs through the ceiling. "Yes . . . I'll take it up in a minute," she said, sounding unsure of herself as she carried it out into the hall. Celia saw her look up again before placing it on the step at the bottom of the stairs. When Lauren came back into the room, she was smiling. "There now. I'll remember where I left it this time."

As Lauren sat down on the sofa all eyes were on her, and the silence in the room became awkward. Celia broke the spell by saying, "Let's play a game. Trivia, anyone?"

"On a Tuesday?" Robert asked. "My brain only works on weekends."

Susan giggled.

"Poker?" Celia asked. "Monopoly? Go Fish?"

"How about the Ouija board?" Susan exclaimed as if she had only now noticed it.

"Not that." Lauren looked as startled as if she really had forgotten it was there.

"Why not?" Susan insisted. "I think it would be fun."

"Sounds good to me," Robert seconded.

Both Celia and Lauren turned and stared at him. Celia was sure Robert had been opposed to using it before. Her eyes thoughtfully narrowed. She had seen several glances and smiles between Susan and Robert, but she had discounted them because she knew they worked together. However, this evening they also had arrived together. Was it a coincidence, or had they ridden over in the same car? Celia felt a surge of anger toward Robert. True, Lauren had been behaving oddly of late, but she and Robert had an understanding, as it was quaintly called in Siddel Marsh. Susan had no right to interfere.

Ignoring Lauren's protest, Susan picked up the Ouija board and handed it to Robert, then pulled up a chair opposite him so that their knees almost touched. Robert set the board between them, resting it on their knees.

"What's this?" Robert said as he turned the planchette upside down and unwound a hair ribbon from its feet. Taking one end of it between his thumb and forefinger, he extended his arm toward Lauren. "I see you went all out on decorating."

She took the satin ribbon from him and stared at it as if she had never seen one before.

"It is yours, isn't it?" Susan asked.

"Yes, of course it's mine." Lauren still looked confused, as she wadded the ribbon into her palm and closed her hand around it.

A moment later, Lauren left the room to put the ribbon on the stairs with her hairbrush, and as she was leaving, Celia covertly watched Susan and Robert exchange a smile. Had Susan somehow managed to put the ribbon there while Celia and Lauren were getting the drinks? And why? Celia had never known Lauren to wear a ribbon in her hair, and she would have said Lauren wasn't the type to even own such a ribbon. But then she also had assumed Lauren would never host a party wearing a worn-out blouse and with her hair pushed up every which way.

Susan and Robert rested their fingers on the planchette. "Is there anybody there?" she called out. Susan's normally soft voice seemed to soar up through the floors above and around the stairwell. Celia shook her head impatiently at her flight of imagination.

The triangle of wood began to move sluggishly, stopping at random letters.

"Who are you?" Susan asked.

Again the pointer swung aimlessly around the board.

"That doesn't spell anything," Mark observed. "Maybe you contacted an illiterate spirit."

Susan grimaced at him. "You have to take this seriously, or there's no telling what sort of spirit we might contact."

"Oh, right." Mark winked at Celia.

After several more tries Robert gave up. "This is silly."

"Maybe it's because you've had some Scotch." Susan seemed to be enjoying being the expert in the room. "Sometimes alcohol can affect psychic happenings."

"I should think booze would enhance it," Mark said with a laugh.

Robert grinned as if to say he agreed.

"Celia, you try it," Susan urged.

"No, not me." For some reason Celia felt an

aversion to putting her hands on that board. She didn't even want the board sitting on her lap.

"I'll try," Lauren said as she stood and smoothed her black skirt in a nervous gesture.

As Lauren took Robert's seat, Celia thought she looked as grim as if she were about to engage in a game to the death. She put her slender fingers opposite Susan's, the frayed spot on her cuff visible to all.

"Eenie, meanie, chili beanie," Mark mocked, as if he were spouting a famous incantation, "the spirits are about to speak."

"Are they friendly spirits?" Robert joined in.

"You two watch too many cartoons," Celia scolded. Both Susan and Lauren seemed upset.

"You try it," Susan urged. "Ask who's there."

"I feel silly."

"It's only a game," Robert reminded her. "You act as if you believe in this stuff."

"Ask," Susan commanded in a soft voice.

"All right, all right. Who's there?"

At once the planchette began to swing in wide, firm arcs. Deliberately it spelled, "W E L..."

"What's that word? Welcome?" Mark leaned forward and Celia handed him a pen and paper from her purse. "'Welcome...to...my... house.' Thank you, Lauren. We're glad to be here."

"I'm not doing it," Lauren snapped. "Susan is."

"Me?" Susan exclaimed. "It's not *my* house."
She stared down at the board. "Who are you?"

The pointer swung to the N.

"N A T H A..." Mark repeated as he wrote
what the pointer indicated.

"That's not funny," Lauren exclaimed as she
jerked her fingers off the planchette and glared
at Susan. "Why are you doing this to me?" Her
voice rose as she jumped to her feet.

"Me? What am I doing?" Susan looked genuinely puzzled.

"That's enough, Lauren," Robert snapped.

"She's deliberately trying to scare me."

Robert went to Susan and took her arm. "I
think we had better be going."

Lauren's mouth dropped open as she stared
from one to the other. "You two came together?" Her voice squeaked on the last word.

"We live in the same neighborhood," Susan
hastily defended. "I offered him a ride."

"I knew I wouldn't be staying late," Robert
added. "It is a Tuesday, after all."

Lauren looked stunned.

"I'll see them out," Celia offered, hoping to
defuse what could be an unpleasant scene.

When she reached the door with Robert and
Susan, Celia glared at them. "You could have
handled this more tactfully," she hissed. "I
can't believe you would be so cruel to poor
Lauren."

"Listen," Robert whispered back, "she
doesn't own me. Sure, we've dated for a long
time, but we aren't married."

Celia gave him a poisonous look. "Good night, Robert. Susan."

She shut the door behind them and stalked back to the drawing room. If Robert wanted to cool his relations with Lauren, he should have been courteous enough to tell her so privately and not to publicly embarrass her. She was fuming with righteous indignation when she went back into the room.

Lauren was sitting on the sofa, a small lace handkerchief in her hands.

Celia thought this was too melodramatic until Lauren said, "I found this on the mantel."

"Where did it come from?"

"It's a lace handkerchief that belonged to my grandmother. It's supposed to be upstairs in my cedar chest."

"It's lovely. It goes with your blouse."

Lauren looked miserably from Celia to Mark. "I didn't bring it down here."

"You must have."

Lauren shook her head.

"Handkerchiefs don't walk around on their own," Mark reminded her.

"Neither do hairbrushes or ribbons," Lauren said. "I was using the hairbrush upstairs just before you two came. I never saw the ribbon before, at least not that I recall."

Celia smiled. "You must have absently brought the brush down with you and dropped it in the chair. Cushions are notorious about eating things."

"I wouldn't come through here from upstairs

to answer the front door. I always use the main stairs, not the servant's steps."

"I didn't know there were any other stairs."

"They go from a broom closet in the kitchen up to the extra closet in the Summer room. I guess from there they go to the servant's room in the attic, but I've never looked."

"At any rate, there's a logical explanation for all of this."

"Yes, there is. I believe someone else is in my house."

Celia felt a chill run down her spine. "That's impossible!"

"Is it? Even the locksmith said someone fixed my broken lock. I'm always hearing noises."

"It's an old house," Mark reminded her. "As for the lock, the man must have been mistaken. Maybe it was repaired before you bought the house."

Lauren's eyes went back to the Ouija board. "I can't believe Susan would be so cruel."

"Neither can I," Celia agreed.

"You know what she was spelling, don't you? Nathaniel." When Celia and Mark looked confused, Lauren added, "Nathaniel Padgett. He owned this house until he died. She was deliberately trying to frighten me."

"Oh." Celia didn't know what else to say. Lauren seemed determined to pretend the embarrassing display of attention between her supposed fiancé and Susan hadn't happened. Maybe the shock of learning that Robert and

Susan had not only had a date but had come as a couple to her own party was more than Lauren could handle. That would explain why she kept talking about her fears.

"We could help you search the house," Mark suggested. "We can prove to you there's no one here but us."

Lauren looked relieved. "Would you? I know it sounds silly, but . . ."

"Let's do it," Celia quickly agreed. "Should we start at the top or the bottom?"

They started in the attic and methodically worked their way down. By the time they finished, the hem of Lauren's long skirt was rimmed with dust and Celia was sneezing.

"See? Nothing here." Mark grinned at Lauren. "No ghosties, no ghoulies, no nothing."

"Thank you both. I feel so foolish to have put you through all this."

"Think nothing of it."

Celia looked at her watch. "Can it really be this late? We have to go. We all have to work tomorrow."

Lauren also checked her mantel clock. "Nearly midnight? Already?" She felt a vague disorientation. Could they have spent so long in going through the house? Was it possible? At least the others were aware of a loss of time as well. It wasn't only her this time.

She saw them out and locked the door. She was alone in the house. This time she knew it was true. No prowler could have evaded them all.

She went to the stairs to get the brush and ribbon so she could take them up and put them away, but they weren't where she had left them. Fear seized her for a moment, making the tiny hairs on the nape of her neck stand on end, but then it occurred to her that Celia must have put them away for her. Drawing a deep breath, Lauren calmed herself. No one else was in the house; she was sure.

As she usually did these days, Lauren left all the lights on as she went upstairs. Maybe, she thought with sudden inspiration, the lights were wired to an automatic timer and were programed to turn themselves off in sequence.

When she reached the top of the stairs, the entire house was suddenly plunged into darkness. With a stifled scream Lauren felt for the flashlight she had left on a small table at the head of the stairs, but she couldn't find it in the dark. Her hands outstretched, she groped for her door and the light switch within.

Soft fingers closed over her wrist as she touched the switch and gently drew her hand away. Panic seized her, and she was unable to breathe, let alone scream.

All at once all the lights simultaneously came back on. A quick look around verified she was alone in the room.

Although her heart was still pounding, she found she wasn't quite as frightened as much as she was startled. It was as if—whatever— had sensed her fear and turned the lights back on to reassure her.

She looked down at her wrist. The touch—even though it had to have been in her imagination—had been gentle. She spread her fingers over the spot, but hers felt smaller than the ones she had felt in the dark. The hand had been much larger, like a man's hand. Obviously, however, no one was there.

She found it surprising on one level that she wasn't afraid anymore. It was as if this were a time-out, a cocoon of peace from the rest of the harried world. She felt protected. The faint scent of cloves filled the room as she prepared for bed.

Chapter Eight

Lauren sat bolt upright in bed as it all came back to her. Why hadn't she been afraid? Something had grabbed her wrist, for God's sake!

She turned on her bedside lamp and looked at the clock. 5:00 A.M. At some point during the night the lights had gone back off again, leaving the upper foyer and stairs in blackness.

Nervously she looked around the room. The hairbrush and ribbon were on her nightstand where Celia must have put them. Beside them, folded into a neat square, was her grandmother's lace handkerchief. Lauren didn't remember putting it there, but much of last night had seemed like a dream.

Robert! He had brought that horrid Susan

Redlow to the party, as if she were a date. Lauren had half a mind to go downstairs, call him up and demand to know what was going on, but the utter blackness of the stairwell convinced her to wait. She would see them both at work in a few hours, and they had better have a convincing reason for arriving in the same car.

She knew sleep was out of the question, so she got out of bed and wandered over to the window. With the lamp on, she couldn't see the lake so she went into the blue room, carefully making her way through the darkness there with the aid of the faint moonlight penetrating the windows. Of course, there was little in the blue room to avoid bumping into as the only furniture there was the enormous sleigh bed.

From the windows surrounding the turret area of the room, she looked out as though she had been drawn to do so. Although the moon was no longer completely full, it was still reflecting enough light for her to see the lake, laying like molten silver, and the woods, which formed a black velvet border around its shores. In the faint light, the marshy areas of the lake looked safe and firm. Moonbeams washed the tops of the trees in silver.

Lauren stared down at the lake. It was so serene, so peaceful. She wished with all her heart that she had that serenity for herself. At times the world seemed to spin so quickly that she couldn't keep up with all she had to do.

Women might be liberated, she reflected, but in doing so they had added a lot of stress. She might someday be a full partner at Newton and Combe, but she had to give up a lot as well. Women might have felt overburdened over having to run a household and raise children, but Lauren had all that in her future plus a full-time job.

The light breeze rippled the lake's surface as if answering in sympathy.

Life was simply too hard. All she had ever wanted, really, was someone to take care of her.

She considered going down to the lake and wading in its shallows. At this time of night no one would see her in her nightgown.

She went to the bedroom door and looked into the foyer's darkness. No, it was much too fearfully dark. No moonlight touched that inner foyer and stairs. Lauren closed the door and went back through the interconnecting door to her own room. Leaving the lamp on, she lay down, and was asleep before her head had barely touched the pillow.

"Young lady, you said our blueprints would be ready today."

"I know, Mr. Flournoy, but something came up." Lauren had another of her splitting headaches, and his shouting was making it worse.

"Look," his wife chimed in. "She's still got that blasted well stuck in the middle of the kitchen."

"I can fix that." Lauren grabbed a bottle of white type-eraser and globbed some over the well symbol. "There, now the damned thing is gone!"

"Don't you yell at me!" Mrs. Flournoy shouted.

"Don't you yell at my wife!" her husband cried out in unison with her.

Lauren sat back in her chair and rubbed ineffectively at her forehead. "I'm sorry. I apologize, but—"

"No buts about it. If Newton and Combe can't give us a competent architect, we'll go somewhere else."

"Perhaps if I try again," Lauren suggested. "I could start all over with a new idea. Maybe a quaint little cottage with gingerbread details on the porch, or—"

"Cottage! Gingerbread! Hell, no! We want an A-frame. With solid glass at each end."

"And one of those red iron fireplaces like they have in Sweden," his wife added.

Lauren suppressed a shudder. "Anyone can have one of those houses. I was trying to give you something unique."

"Yeah, a well in the kitchen may be unique," Mr. Flournoy said, making the word sound distasteful, "but we don't want that. Damn it, we want what we paid for. An A-frame with lots of glass."

Mrs. Flournoy nodded emphatically.

Following a discreet knock at the door, Robert looked in. "Is there a problem?"

"No," Lauren said.

"I'd say there is," Mr. Flournoy objected with a withering look at her. "We can't get Miss Hamilton here to draw up our house plans."

"Oh?" Robert came in and shut the door behind him. "What exactly seems to be the trouble?"

"We want an A-frame," Mrs. Flournoy spoke up. "A modern house with all the fancy trimmings. Miss Hamilton is determined to build us one more suitable to...to my grandmother."

"Is this true?" Robert asked Lauren.

Lauren sighed and touched the brooch at her throat. She was wearing the pale yellow blouse she had bought at the same time as the white one. Until the Flournoys had arrived, she had felt particularly good about herself.

"It even has a blasted well in the kitchen," Mrs. Flournoy added. "A well!"

Robert leaned over the drawing and touched the damp white spot. "A well?" His dark eyes glared at Lauren.

"I erased it. Okay?"

"This still isn't an A-frame," Robert pointed out. "It's some sort of cottage."

"With the right touches it would be adorable," Lauren said. "It could be one of the best I've done. Their lot is heavily wooded, and this cottage would look terrific on it."

"But it's their lot," Robert hissed, "and their

house. Are you actually refusing to design the house they want?''

Lauren knew he was giving her one last chance to salvage this account. "I've been meaning to ask you," she said bluntly, "are you seeing Susan Redlow behind my back?"

At the sound of sharply indrawn breaths, she realized she shouldn't have blurted it out like that with others in the room, but no gentleman would accuse her of not doing good work, especially in front of the clients she was trying to work with. She was glad she had embarrassed him. Let it be on his own conscience.

"I apologize for Miss Hamilton," Robert said smoothly to the couple. "If you'll come into my office, I'll try to work this out." He guided them to the door, and they seemed all too eager to leave the room. Behind their backs he scowled at Lauren as he said to them, "I have an entire portfolio of A-frames, and I'm positive I can modify one to suit you." He shut the door behind them.

Lauren stiffly sat in the silence. Robert had stolen her clients. He had actually walked in and whisked them away, and just when she had almost convinced them to go with her cottage design. Angrily she crumpled the sketches she'd done and threw them in the wastebasket. She was too talented to waste her time on people who could not see the possibilities in her work.

She stood up and went to the hat tree to get her bonnet. It was new and exactly the shade of her dark green skirt, and it had a tiny veil, held back with a pearl pin. It was perfect for a working woman to wear on the street from house to office.

When she went out into the front desk area, Susan looked up in surprise. Lauren wasn't sure how much she had heard of the commotion in her office, but she sincerely hoped she had caught Lauren's scathing accusation to Robert.

"Are you going somewhere? It's not lunchtime yet."

Lauren swept by her. "I have to see a man about a dog." She almost could have laughed at the expression on Susan's face. Let her explain why Newton and Combe were missing an architect!

As Lauren got in her car, she decided the idea of a dog wasn't a bad one. She could certainly use a watch dog.

She drove to a small building which sat at the edge of town, looking as welcoming as a prison. The man behind the desk, looking as though he might be the humane society's only employee, stood up as Lauren entered. "Can I help you?"

"I want a dog—not a puppy, but a full-grown one. For a watchdog," she added.

"I think I've got just the one."

He led her through a back door and into the side yard that held the dogs. The whines and barks and yelps made her headache worse, but Lauren kept walking. The puppy kennels were closest to the door, and the dog runs were in the back.

"We got this one in last week," the man said. "He belonged to the folks that had that car lot over on Maple Street. They took off owing everybody in town and left their dog behind. Some folks do that. Trash, I call 'em."

Lauren looked through the wire mesh at the dog. He was big, a mix between shepherd, doberman, and something that resembled a mastiff. He regarded her with a steady stare. "Is he a good watchdog?"

The man chuckled. "He sure is. It took me and my men all day to get him out of that junkyard and into this pen."

"He sounds vicious. I don't want one that will hurt me."

"No, he ain't mean." The man unlatched the door to the pen and stepped in. The dog wagged his stump of a tail. "See? He's just trained to protect his territory. When you get home, lead him all around your yard and let him mark his boundaries. Do it several times. That way he knows what's his."

"I don't have a fence."

"That's a problem. He has to be penned."

"Is he housebroken? I could keep him inside until I have a fence put up."

"I don't know if he is or not, but I reckon you could train him. He seems right smart."

"I'll take him. What's his name?"

"One of my men said he thought it was King. The dog seems to know that name."

"All right, King, you're my dog now." Lauren was gratified to see his ears prick forward. She wondered why she hadn't thought of this before.

She paid for King's shots, and the man gave her a length of rope to use as a leash. King still wore a thick leather collar that looked as tough as he did.

King obediently jumped into the back seat of her car, and as she slipped behind the steering wheel, she could hear him panting. She tried not to think of those massive jaws of his so close to her neck.

When she reached her house, she could hear her phone ringing, but she ignored it and began leading King around the perimeter of her yard. Whether he would bite or not, she thought his appearance alone was enough to scare a prowler half to death.

After making several circles of the yard, Lauren led King toward the back door, but the closer they got to the house, the slower he moved. "Come on, King." She pulled harder on the leash, and reluctantly he followed her up the porch steps and waited for her to open the door. He showed no signs of wanting to pass over the threshold.

Lauren dragged him into the kitchen and patted him while he looked around suspiciously. She filled a bowl with water and, not having any dog food, fed him the leftovers from her supper the night before. King wolfed down the food and sat back on his haunches.

"Come see the rest of the house," Lauren said. "Come on. Heel."

King slunk along behind her, his large head swinging from side to side.

"What's the matter? Aren't you used to being inside?" she asked as she patted him again. "It's air-conditioned. With all your hair, you'll love it."

She had to haul him through the drawing room, but he outran her getting out of the library. Lauren was beginning to wonder if he was too cowardly to be a watchdog. Maybe the man at the animal shelter had sold her a bill of goods.

The phone started ringing again, but as before she ignored it. No doubt it would be Robert with more unpleasant accusations about her not being at work. She didn't feel like explaining her every move to him.

After much pushing and shoving, she was able to get the dog started up the stairs, but once he was moving, he didn't stop until he had reached the attic. On the top landing, he stopped and looked back at her.

"You want to start up there? Okay. It's up to you."

Personally she thought the attic was the creepiest place in the house, but here King ranged away from her, his nose curiously snuffling every corner.

After they had completed the circuit of the attic, she had to drag him back downstairs. King walked with stiff-legged reluctance until they reached the blue room. There he balked and, throwing back his head, gave a blood-curdling howl. The sound chilled Lauren to the bone. "Stop that! Be quiet!" The dog lowered his head but continued to whine.

Lauren shut the door to the bedroom, and King almost knocked her down in his eagerness to go downstairs. He went straight to the front door and scratched to be let out.

"No, King. You've got to get used to being inside, at least until I can have the yard fenced."

She went back to the kitchen, and he padded after her as if he were afraid to be left alone. Lauren washed the bowl she had put the food scraps in and wondered how much a dog that size would eat. That was one of the questions she should have asked.

When her doorbell rang, King emitted a low, meanacing growl, his muscled body instantly alert.

"Good boy," Lauren said with approval. "Maybe you really are a watchdog after all."

Together they went to the door. "Celia! I didn't expect you. Come in and have some iced tea."

"Iced tea? Lauren, what the hell is going on? Robert called me and . . ." She caught sight of King and froze. "What's that?" she whispered.

"This is King, my new watch dog. Isn't he great?"

"That's enough to scare the socks off anyone. Does he bite?"

"You're safe with me here." Lauren enjoyed saying that. It made her feel safe as well as in control. "Let's go into the drawing room."

"I can't stay. I'm on my lunch break. Lauren, why did you leave work without telling anyone? Robert says you did that yesterday, too. And that there's some problem between some clients and yourself?"

"Robert worries too much. He's mainly upset because I asked if he's seeing Susan."

Celia looked at her closely. "What did he say?"

"He pretended not to hear me. Let me fix you a sandwich. It won't take but a minute."

"No, really, I can't. Are you going back to work this afternoon?"

"I haven't decided."

"You haven't . . . Lauren, what's the matter with you? You *have* to work. From the way Robert sounded, you're right on the verge of being fired."

"Robert is practically a full partner, and he won't allow them to fire me." Lauren laughed at the idea. "I'm tired of having to draw up house plans that are as dull as dishwater. Isn't anybody interested in charm anymore?"

"He didn't go into details with me. It's none of my business."

"True," Lauren agreed.

Celia shot her a questioning look. "He wants me to find out what's going on with you and get you to straighten out."

"Nothing is wrong with me. What could possibly be wrong?"

Celia looked at her more closely. "Is that what you wore to work today?"

"Yes. Do you like it? I got this blouse the same day I bought my white one."

"You wore the hat, too?" Celia was conspicuously staring at her.

"That's right. I think it's cute. If you like, I'll loan it to you." She removed the hat and hung it on the hall tree.

"I don't know what's going on, but I think you need a vacation."

"A what?" Lauren asked with a laugh.

"I'll take care of your . . . dog. I'm sure I can convince Robert to give you a couple of weeks off."

"Nonsense. I don't want to go anywhere. I love it here."

"In Siddel Marsh? You were never all that fond of it before."

"No, here. In my house."

Celia looked around as if the house made her uneasy. "Yeah, well, that's peculiar, too. I mean, this place reminds me of a set from *Psycho*."

Lauren drew herself up. "There's no need to be rude."

"I'm sorry. Really I am. I just don't understand the changes I see in you. I'm worried because you're my friend, and I care about you."

Lauren patted Celia on the shoulder. "You're

getting all worked up over nothing. I'm fine."

"How do you expect me to believe that? You don't dress the same or talk the same. It's like you're turning into someone else."

Lauren laughed. "Doesn't that sound pretty ridiculous? Do you want to search my attic for pods from outer space?"

Celia had to laugh. "I guess that did sound stupid. I don't know what it is. You're just different."

"Everybody changes. Nothing stays exactly the same."

"Of course not. Just don't change too much. Okay? I liked the old Lauren." She turned to leave. "What should I tell Robert?"

"Tell him to stop seeing Susan, and that I'll be waiting for him when he comes to his senses."

"I can't tell him that. What should I say about work?"

Lauren waved her hand in a vague gesture. "Tell him I'm working on some plans at home. I don't have any clients due in this afternoon."

"Okay." Celia paused. "Is it true? *Are* you working?"

"Certainly."

Lauren waited behind the closed door until Celia got into her car and drove away. "She's becoming tedious," she told the dog. "Otherwise, I would have invited her over for dinner later."

She went upstairs, leaving the dog behind. If Robert called, she wanted to say she had been working. She had never been good at lying.

Lauren had put her drafting table and paper in the green room where she would not be able to see the lake, because she found that view too mesmerizing and distracting. Idly she ruffled through her folio. Somehow she had managed to get behind on quite a few assignments. Mixed in with sketches and blueprints were list after list of ideas pertaining to her house. She pulled these out and filed them separately. For a minute she stopped and thought about those lists. She had never been one to make lists. She had always carried everything in her head.

"Making lists is much more efficient," she said aloud to herself. "It's amazing that I never did it before, not vice versa."

She sat down at the drafting table and took out an almost finished blueprint for a new, downtown building. As she studied it, she could see where a few touches here and there would transform it from an ordinary, unexciting box of a building to one with a unique charm. She made quick sketches. With a little luck she might even be able to locate some of the old pneumatic tubes and the brass canisters that traveled in them. And ceiling fans. And a pressed metal ceiling! Feverish excitement overtook her, and her pencil skimmed over the paper.

The first crash made her jump so hard that she broke the pencil lead. Then came the frenzied howls that made her hair stand on end.

Lauren threw down her pencil and ran for the stairs. "King? King!"

She was afraid of what she might find. Was he rabid or crazy? Why had she trusted a stranger to sell her such a potentially vicious dog?

She could hear King snarling, as if he was ready to attack, and she headed down the stairs. Had Celia returned and foolishly come into the house? No, that was unlikely; she had heard no human screams. Then the snarls became punctuated by nerve-jangling howls and whines.

Lauren reached the hallway at the bottom of the stairs in time to see King tear out of the parlor, his eyes rolling in terror. He skidded on the oak floor as if trying desperately to find his footing. The front door swung open, and he went barreling out.

Lauren stood there with her mouth open. The dog was gathering speed as he crossed the lawn and disappeared into the bushes that separated her yard from that of her neighbors. His howls died in the distance.

The front door swung shut.

"Who are you?" Lauren whispered. Then more desperately, "Who *are* you?"

There was no answer, and she really hadn't expected one.

Chapter Nine

Lauren put a smile on her face as she went to answer the door. Sunlight touched the silver cross she wore at her neck.

"I came about the room?" the man said doubtfully. "I'm Joseph Dodd."

"I'm Lauren Hamilton," she responded as she sized up her perspective boarder. He was old enough to be respectable but young enough for interesting conversation.

He remained standing on the porch. "Where is the place you're renting out?"

"Why, it's right upstairs. Won't you come in?"

Dodd stepped inside and looked around. "Isn't this the old Padgett place?"

"Yes, it is." She smiled again.

"I've never been inside before. I grew up near here. Used to ride by it on my bicycle."

"It's rather large as you can see." She started to precede him upstairs. "That's why I decided to take in a boarder. It's so big." She looked over her shoulder. "It's up here. Are you coming?"

Dodd looked startled and began to follow her. "You live here alone?"

"At the moment," she said evasively. After all, she didn't know this man. "I expect to be married soon."

They reached the foyer, and she said, "It's this room here." She pushed open the door to the red room. "It's called the Summer room because of the color."

He stepped inside and looked around doubtfully. "Do you plan to rent it as it is, or will you be doing some decorating?"

Lauren looked up at the age-stained wallpaper. She hadn't noticed before that the room needed so much work. "I can rent it cheaper if you do the repairs yourself. Are you handy with a paintbrush, Mr. Dodd?"

"No, that's why I rent instead of own. I don't know, Miss Hamilton. It's not what I expected."

"You'd have your privacy," she assured him quickly. "See? Here are some private stairs that lead down to the kitchen. Your bathroom is behind that door. It shares with the Spring room, but since no one lives in it, it's very quiet."

He poked his head into the stair closet and looked up. "What's up there?"

"Only the attic. I believe this stairway leads to a small room that was used by a servant."

"You don't know for sure?"

"The room is unused. I never needed to find out what it was used for." That sounded peculiar to her, too, but she couldn't admit she was afraid to go up and look.

"I don't know." He went back in the room and looked around. "It needs a lot of work."

Lauren tried to see the room from Dodd's point of view. The carpet was as faded as the wallpaper, and there were worn spots in the floral pattern in the traffic areas. The curtains looked dark and heavy and dusty. There was a tear in one of the lace sheers, and the windows were grimy. "It has character, and it's nice and big. There would be no problem in it accommodating even a large bedroom suite. You do have your own furniture, don't you? The ad specified it was unfurnished."

"Yes," he said absently, "I have my own things. This wasn't Old Man Padgett's room by any chance, was it?"

"I don't think so. The Winter room on the opposite corner seems to have been the master bedroom. My room adjoins this, but I'll install a lock on both sides of the door for privacy—and I can assure you I'm a quiet person."

"Do you have pets? I'm allergic to animals."

"Not any more."

"I'm allergic to dust, too," he added as he

looked around the room. "And mold."

"I assure you there is no mold here," Lauren replied in a cool voice. "Do you want the room or not?"

"I don't think so." He glanced about uneasily. "No, it won't suit me."

She followed him downstairs. "If it's the amount of rent..."

"No, no. That's not it." He hesitated at the doorway. "To tell you the truth, it's the house itself. I didn't know you were renting a room in it, or I wouldn't have applied. I assumed it was over the garage or maybe something out back."

"What's wrong with my house?" Ice dripped from her words.

"Not a thing, Miss Hamilton. But, well, Old Man Padgett was an odd one, a real strange sort."

"Perhaps, but he's dead now."

The man nodded but looked around as if he expected the dead man to make an appearance. "All the same, I think I'd better turn it down. Maybe you'll have better luck with a newcomer to town." He turned and hurried out to his car.

Lauren slammed the door after him. He was wrong. Even strangers to the town were leery of renting in this house. She knew because she had tried to rent the room all month. Dozens of people had looked at it, some she suspected out of curiosity, but no one wanted to live there.

Lauren went into the parlor and automatically straightened the mirror for the third time that day. On the sofa in a neat pile were all her wash cloths. She sat beside them and sighed. She never knew where she would find anything these days.

At first she thought she was moving the things herself. Often she had lapses of time when hours passed unaccountably. So she had rigged a net of string that no one could step over or avoid, but the things continued to move. She might find a vase sitting in the middle of the floor, a single rose slanted in it. Or a book might appear on her kitchen cabinet. Or her skillet might show up in the bathtub. It didn't matter if it was day or night, but things seemed to stay in place more regularly if someone else was in the house. That was why she had begun trying to find a boarder.

A knock at the door drew her attention, and she stood up eagerly. Maybe Dodd had had second thoughts. She hurried to the door and opened it to find Celia on her porch.

"I hope you haven't eaten yet. I put together some sandwiches."

"Come in." Lauren smiled at her friend. "I can't tell you how much I appreciate you sticking by me like this."

"That's what friends are for. Do you have a date with Robert tonight?"

Lauren avoided her eyes. "He has to work tonight."

"On a Saturday?"

"I don't believe it, either."

When they entered the kitchen Celia went to a book that was lying open on the table. "What are you reading?"

Lauren looked at it as if it were a snake. "I'm not. It wasn't there a few minutes ago."

Celia gave her a measured look and read the title. "*Sonnets To the Portuguese*. Romantic."

"I told you I'm not reading it. I don't even like poems."

Celia paused. "So what's it doing here?"

"I've told you. Things show up all over the house. I never know where I'll find anything."

"'How do I love thee ...'" Celia read.

"I don't want to hear it."

Celia closed the book and rested her fingers on it. "Maybe you should talk to a doctor. I'll go with you if you're afraid to go alone."

"There's nothing wrong with me."

"Stress can—"

"Stress be damned! I'm not imagining these things." Lauren sat wearily at the table. "Why won't anyone believe me?"

Celia rested her hand on Lauren's shoulder. "I don't know what to say."

Lauren felt a ridiculous urge to cry, even though she never cried. Naturally Celia didn't believe her. Before she moved to Four Seasons, Lauren wouldn't have believed it either.

"Have you considered moving?" Celia asked.

"Moving? This is my house." At the expression on Celia's face, Lauren added, "I've thought about it."

"Well?"

"To tell you the truth, I can't afford to move. I talked to a couple of realtors, but they said the seller's market is soft right now. When I told them which house I live in, one realtor actually laughed, and the other said it would be easier to sell snowballs in hell."

"She said that?"

"It's what she meant."

"Maybe they're wrong."

"No, I checked, and this house had been on the market for a year before I bought it. Besides, I love this house. I can't explain it, Celia, but it was as if I came home when I moved in here."

"It's just a house, and you obviously aren't happy here." Celia thought for a minute and added, "I could drive you to a doctor in Shreveport, and no one here would ever know."

"I'm perfectly capable of driving myself to a shrink, *if* I needed one. I'm not crazy."

"I never said you were."

Lauren frowned at her. "You've been here when I've found things in odd places. You know I'm not lying."

Celia made no comment.

"Once Robert and I are married all this will straighten itself out. You'll see."

"Are you still so sure you and Robert are getting married?"

Lauren gave a shaky laugh. "Why, of course we are. I bought a quilt for our bed. Do you want to see it?"

"The blue snowflake one? You showed it to me several weeks ago."

"Has it been that long?" She rubbed her forehead nervously. "I have such a headache I can't think straight."

"That's another reason you should go to see a doctor."

"Don't be silly. It's only a headache. I'll go up soon and bathe my temples with rose water. That sometimes works."

"So do aspirin."

Lauren looked at her blankly, then nodded. "Of course. That, too."

Celia went to a wicker basket with garlic piled in it. "Are you on a pasta binge? What do you do with so much garlic?"

Lauren shrugged. "I thought it might help."

"Garlic? And that's a silver cross around your neck. Good heavens, Lauren, you surely don't believe in vampires, do you?"

"Certainly not. But I've tried everything else, and nothing seems to help." She picked up the book of poems and leafed through it listlessly. "Did I tell you I found another rose yesterday? This one was lying on a shelf in the refrigerator." She laughed shakily. "If this were a movie I'd say that someone is trying to make contact." She sighed and shoved the book aside. "But it's not a movie, and I'm starting to get really scared."

"Move out," Celia urged. "You can move in with me until you find another place."

"Listen," Lauren whispered. "See how quiet

the house became? It does that sometimes."

"I don't hear anything different."

"I have a better idea. You move in here."

"What?" Celia gave a little laugh as if that were impossible.

"Don't you see? It would be perfect. You could have the red room and have your own little staircase. We could take turns cooking. What do you say?"

"Lauren, I can't move in here. I have another year's lease on my place."

"So? You wanted me to move in with you. Leases can be broken."

"Thanks, but no thanks. My house is closer to town, and I don't want to move."

"Neither do I." Lauren stood and went to gaze out the back window. "There are times when I get a breeze blowing across the lake, and I smell the wisterias and believe this is the most perfect place in the world."

"Wisterias? In the middle of the summer?"

Lauren didn't answer. After a while she said softly, "Some things, like the flowers and this book of poems, are so romantic. It's almost as if I have a secret admirer."

"What?"

Lauren gave herself a mental shake. "Did you say something?"

"No, you did. Look, I know you think I'm butting into your business, but you're my friend and I'm worried about you."

"That's very sweet of you, but I'm perfectly safe here."

Celia felt a thrill of apprehension. "Only a few minutes ago you said you were scared."

"How silly! You misunderstood me." Lauren leaned her head against the window frame, her mouth tilting up in a smile. "I'm thinking of buying wicker lawn furniture. Don't you think that would look lovely under the oak tree? White wicker, of course. Black or brown is so dreary."

Celia frowned. Lauren not only sounded different, more southern and indolent, but she even appeared different, as if she were smaller with darker hair. "Have you colored your hair?"

"What?" Lauren turned to look at her, and the illusion was gone. "I've considered it. I actually found some gray hairs this morning." She sighed unhappily. "God, I hate the idea of getting old."

"They say it's better than the alternative."

"The lake looks so cool."

Celia was becoming used to Lauren's abrupt switches in conversation. "Yes, it does. You have a beautiful view of it from here."

Lauren made no reply.

"Do you still think someone else has a key to the house?"

"No. I'd have seen them around by now—unless it's Robert. Do you think it's Robert?"

"Why him?"

"Who else would leave me flowers and love poems? Those are gifts from a lover."

"Will you stop with the lover nonsense?"

"Nothing else makes any sense at all."

"Neither does that. Why would Robert put a skillet in your bathtub?"

"To get my attention?"

Celia went to the window and studied Lauren as she gazed at the lake. "You don't really believe that, do you?"

"I don't know what to believe any more." She held up her finger. "Listen to the house. It's not silent any more."

"Would you stop that? You're giving me the creeps."

"Sorry."

"How are things going at work?"

"I don't know. I don't seem to be able to please anyone these days. I turn out perfectly good plans—some I'd say are unusually good— and no one likes them. Except Robert. He has all the faith in the world in me."

Celia turned her worried eyes to gaze out the window. She had talked to Robert and knew this wasn't so. Robert was as worried about Lauren as Celia was, but his way of dealing with it was to retreat. It was only due to Celia's intervention that he was still friendly toward Lauren and was keeping her on at work. Celia had managed to convince him that firing Lauren or not taking her out occasionally might be enough to send her over the edge. She didn't know, however, how long Robert could or would be patient. "Have you ever considered dating someone else?"

"What an idea!"

"Don't laugh. There are plenty of good-looking men around here. Why tie yourself down to one?"

"Why, we're engaged to be married. I can't be unfaithful to Robert." Her expression was as worried as if Celia had suggested they commit a crime.

"It was just an idea."

"Celia, there is something I've been wanting to ask you. Will you be my maid of honor?"

"Maid of honor?"

"Please say you will. I don't have a sister or any female cousins, you know."

"It seems rather premature for you to be planning a wedding, don't you think?" Celia hedged.

"That's the mistake so many people make. They put off planning until the last minute and end up throwing everything together willy-nilly."

"Willy-nilly?"

"I've made lists," Lauren said excitedly. "I have everything down on paper. Robert is sure to want Mark to be his best man. Do you think Mark will do it?"

"I don't—"

"I'll ask him. I have put the Rose Garden Flower Shop down to do the flowers. I think they do lovely work, don't you? And they have the trellises and candle holders and all. I thought twelve candles on either side to symbolize the months of the years and four big fat ones on the alter because the house is Four Seasons."

She waited for Celia to exclaim over her in-genuity.

"You haven't called the flower shop, have you?"

"I did, but they said they couldn't book anything until we set the date."

"For Pete's sake, Lauren, you can't go around calling people like this. What will Robert say?"

"I've tried and tried to reason with him, but you know how men are. He wants to put everything off until the last minute."

"I'll tell you what," Celia bargained. "I'll be your maid of honor, and as such I'll take care of these things for you."

"You will?"

"Absolutely. Just give me the lists and don't worry about a thing."

"Thank you, Celia." Lauren hugged her exuberantly. "You're so good to me. Better even than a sister. This will leave me time to sew my wedding dress."

Celia rolled her eyes to the ceiling and prayed for guidance.

Chapter Ten

On Monday Lauren took off work an hour early and went to the library. Soon she was immersed in the photocopies of newspapers dated 1910. Her eyes burned as she strained to read the blurry print on the illuminated screen. She was so fascinated by the workings of a world that had never heard the terms "World War" or "League of Nations" that she sometimes forgot to search for mention of Nathaniel Padgett or Four Seasons.

In 1910 skirts were still long, though not touching the floor, and were straighter with raised waistlines. Hair was worn in a pompadour or a chignon. Women's hats were enormous and laden with plumes, artificial fruit and stuffed birds. Siddel Marsh's greatest concerns seemed to be whether Taft would be the same quality of president as his predecessor, Teddy Roosevelt, and whether crop prices would rise.

Because she was spending more time reading and less in skimming through the headlines, Lauren came across an article titled, "We Mourn Her Loss." It was about the accidental drowning of Laura Padgett, wife of Nathaniel Padgett.

Lauren blinked and rubbed her eyes before rereading the name. She hadn't suspected Nathaniel's wife would have had a name so close to her own.

Slowly she read the entire article. Laura Padgett had been found dead by her husband. There was no reason, the paper assured, to suspect foul play, although Mrs. Padgett was found in the lake, fully clothed. The popular supposition was that she had fallen into deep water off the end of the pier behind their house, and her heavy skirts had pulled her under.

To Lauren's mind, well trained by television plots and mystery novels, the whole story made no sense. In the first place, clothing wasn't heavy in the water, and the period's straighter skirts meant she would have been wearing fewer petticoats that might have tangled around her legs. Also the lake was close to the house, and if she had screamed, someone would undoubtedly have heard her. Suicide or murder seemed far more likely. Either way her husband could have been at the root of it.

Lauren looked ahead, but aside from a mention of the funeral and the article she had read before about Nathaniel's trip abroad, there was no mention of Laura Padgett.

She turned back to the story about Laura's death and read the date. March 10. Lauren's mouth went dry. That date was familiar to her and with good reason. It was the date of her own birthday.

Lauren sat back in the chair, chiding herself for being foolish. The similarity of names and the date were only coincidences. Nothing more. Laura Padgett had died March 10, 1910, and Lauren Hamilton had been born March 10, 1955. Forty-five years separated the events. She told herself hundreds of other people, some with names similar to hers, had also died on that date in all probability—but none of the others lived at Four Seasons.

Shaken, Lauren turned off the microfilm viewer and replaced the roll of film in its canister. She felt suddenly claustrophobic, as if the library walls were closing in on her. Barely bothering to nod to the librarian, Lauren hurried out.

The heat of the day bore down on her as she fumbled for her car keys. It was all a coincidence. She hadn't been born in Siddel Marsh, and her parents had no connection at all with the Padgetts. As she slid behind the wheel, she wondered what Laura Padgett's maiden name had been and whether there might be another coincidence there. She was afraid to find out.

She drove directly home and parked in the garage but didn't immediately go into the house. Instead she went to the lake and gazed out at the sun-sparkled water. Reluctantly she drew her eyes down to the water's edge and began to search. It didn't take her long to find traces of rotten stumps where the dock's pilings had once stood. Her gaze traveled out over the water. This was where the pier had stood and had been the scene of Laura's death. With a sense of foreboding, she looked back at the house. The turret windows of the blue room were the closest part of the house from this spot. Had Laura also looked up at it just before she jumped off the pier to her death? Or was pushed?

A shiver ran through Lauren, and the unexpected sound of a man's voice caused her to jump.

"Lauren, I know you can hear me, so you might as well answer."

"Robert? What are you doing out here?"

"I've looked all over town for you. Combe is on the warpath over you leaving work early."

"Robert, look at this. See these places? This is where the old pier stood. Laura Padgett drowned at the end of it. And she drowned on March 10th!"

"So what? Lauren, I can't keep covering for you. These past few months you've acted as if you're part-time help instead of a full-time employee. What the hell is going on with you?"

"That's what I'm trying to tell you. Remember what the Ouija board spelled that first night? 'Laura.' That was the name of Padgett's wife."

"So it's similar to yours. Big deal. The name has been around a long time."

"It also spelled 'Welcome home.'"

"Celia was kidding you. After all, it was a housewarming party."

"I know this sounds crazy, but I think Laura Padgett is haunting this house."

Robert looked away as if her words embarrassed him.

"Don't turn away from me. She died March 10th, and that's my birthday."

"Lauren, your imagination is running away with you. So Old Man Padgett's wife had a name similar to yours, and so what if she died on a date that has meaning for you? Life is full of oddities like this. It doesn't mean a thing."

"How can you say that? What about all the things I've found moved around in my house? What about my plants being watered that time and the back lock having been repaired?"

"I never heard of a ghost doing odd jobs around the house."

"What are you saying?"

Robert put his hands on her arms and looked down into her eyes. "Honey, you're imagining all this."

He hadn't called her by a pet name in weeks, but she wasn't interested in that now. "Imagining this? But Celia was here when I found a book of poems open on the table. She can vouch for me finding towels on the stairs and a skillet in my bathtub and—"

"Calm down, Lauren, calm down. There has to be a logical explanation for all this."

"Oh?" she said coolly. "Like what?"

"Maybe you're sleepwalking." When Lauren began to sputter he indignantly added, "People do, you know. These are all things a sleep-walker might do."

"I couldn't repair a lock awake, much less in my sleep."

"Those locks are old and unreliable. It may not have been repaired by anybody but just started working again on its own. That's why newer versions have been invented."

"You think I'm crazy."

"I don't think any such thing." He avoided her eyes.

"You do." Lauren's mouth dropped open in shock. "You really do!"

"Well, damn it, you've been doing some pretty peculiar things lately."

Lauren could only stare at him.

"All this talk about things moving around in your house and showing up in strange places. Not to mention the way you act sometimes."

"What's that supposed to mean?" she demanded.

"I can't explain it. It's like you're another person—different somehow."

"If you ask me, *you're* the one who's crazy."

"Celia has noticed it, too. So have people in the office."

"You've all been getting together to talk about me?" Rage caused her voice to tremble. "How dare you!"

"And there are the sketches and blueprints you've turned in lately. You wait until they're late to start them, which isn't at all like you, and when you finally turn them in, they look like sets from *The Music Man*."

"Why are you insulting me? I demand that you apologize. If I were a man, you'd never dare speak to me thus." A roaring headache blurred her vision, and her tongue feel thick. "I must insist that you leave immediately."

Robert looked as if he were about to say more, but he clamped his mouth shut and strode away.

Lauren glared after him, then turned back to the lake. The water looked so cool and serene, so calming. She swayed toward it.

As she heard Robert's car leave her driveway, her headache lessened. Her anger, however, remained. Robert, Celia and who knew who else had discussed her and decided she was crazy. She stalked toward the house to call Celia and give her a piece of her mind.

She slammed the door behind her and listened with a sense of joy as the sound reverberated throughout the house. Robert was such a cad.

Lauren stopped and thought about that notion. A cad wouldn't have qualms about lying. He might even do so to turn her against her friends so he would be more important in her life. That made sense. Lately she had been too busy to devote the time to Robert that she once had. He was jealous.

A smile tilted the corners of her mouth. She rather liked the idea of a jealous lover. It was so romantic.

Humming "Come, Josephine, in My Flying Machine," she went upstairs to her bedroom to get a pencil and paper, her fingers affectionately trailing over the stair rail. Since she had nothing to do at the moment, she thought she would make a list of items she wanted to purchase for the Winter room.

As she examined the room in greater detail than before, she breathed deeply of the faint clove scent that was ever-present in the house and in this room in particular. The room needed a lot of work, she noticed. The wallpaper was in shreds in some spots near the ceiling. She tore off a corner of wallpaper and put it in her notebook. With luck she might be able to almost match it from a book of wallpaper patterns.

As she ambled around the corner of the L-shaped room and saw the bed, her heart leapt into her throat, and she froze in her tracks. Something white lay on the bed. For one fearful moment, she thought she had discovered Laura Padgett herself. Then reason returned, and she realized it was only a dress. Cautiously she went nearer. Why would she have put a dress in here? And what dress was it? She owned nothing like it.

Carefully, Lauren picked up the dress. It was made entirely of white lace over a white satin undergarment, and it was long and trailing. A wedding dress.

Her headache returned with such force she gasped. The dress blurred for a moment, then came back into focus. She smiled. It was almost finished. The sleeves were pinned in, and it lacked a hem. She had done such a good job on it, not to have had a sewing machine.

Lauren took the pattern from the bed and studied the picture on the front. It was a lovely design. Without the train and in a dark material it would also make a nice day dress. By adding different trim, a bit of lace here, a bow there, she could vary it enough for several dresses. Lauren sat on the side of the bed, took up her needle and began to sew.

Lauren held up the wedding dress and studied it carefully. Her memory threatened to fade away and leave her with more of the blank hours she had come to dread, but she willed it to stay. Vaguely at first, then with more certainty, she recalled sewing on the dress. Although she couldn't imagine why she had chosen to make it, she was relieved to find she could remember the action. Lauren had been taught to sew by one of her aunts, and since she enjoyed needlework, her ability to create the intricate dress was no mystery. But why a wedding dress?

She stood and spread the dress over the bed

so she could get a good look at it. The design was beautiful, with yards of snowy lace and creamy satin and tiny buttons at the bodice and sleeves. A glance at her wristwatch told her she had worked on it most of the night. Her tired muscles bore this out.

Slowly she rubbed her head and forced down her fears. She was going to be married—to Robert. That was why she had sewn the dress. That made sense. She couldn't exactly recall Robert's proposal, but she remembered snatches and bits of conversations about their future marriage.

Lauren went to the turret window and looked out, but with the lamps lit she could see only blackness. That suited her, since she knew she was looking down at the point where the pier had stood. Apprehension suddenly enveloped her like the darkness that shrouded the world around her and she wanted to move away from the window and the pier, but she forced herself to stand there, looking out the window until that fear was conquered as well.

Was there something wrong with her? Robert had seemed to think so. Of course she knew part of that was due to his jealousy, but was there a grain of truth there as well? Celia was also worried. And there were those dreadful headaches. Lauren didn't know what to think of them. Up until a few months ago, she had seldom had a headache in her entire life.

They were migraines. She was sure of it. Over the years Lauren had known other people who had migraines, and they had described a ringing in their ears, blurred vision, even temporary blindness. Even she had had migraines once, during her junior year at college. Yes, the headaches were definitely migraines. Surely a headache so severe that it could cause blindness could also result in temporary amnesia. That made sense to Lauren.

It didn't explain why her belongings showed up in strange places, but it did explain her losses of memory. She recalled having a headache while Robert was there earlier and another after she came upstairs. If she hadn't forced herself to remember, she would have lost the hours she had spent sewing on the wedding dress.

Lauren turned back to look at the dress. She didn't recall Robert agreeing to a wedding date. Maybe the dress wasn't even hers. Could she be making it for Celia? No, she and Mark weren't serious about each other. It was her own dress.

Maybe, she thought, she should see a doctor, just to rule out the possibility of a brain tumor. Maybe it was something as simple as a temporary chemical imbalance or a new allergy to wine or cheese. She had read somewhere that something in wine and cheese could cause migraines. Had she had wine or cheese in the last 24 hours? She wasn't sure, but she told herself there was nothing odd about not being able to recall what she had eaten. Eating was such a habit. And, besides, no one had perfect recall.

She went into the bathroom that accommodated both her room and the blue one, and although the hour was late, she felt the need for a bath. All her muscles were stiff and sore from sitting in one position for so long.

One of the renovations Lauren had made to the house was a shower head in her bathroom. When she had moved in, there were only tubs in both bathrooms, but she occasionally preferred a shower, especially when she was tired from bending over her sketches.

A frown marred her face as she looked back at the open door to the Winter room. A wedding dress! She tried to content herself with the reassurance that she had at least been able to recall sewing on it. She had no idea why she had started it or when she had begun, but those memories might return.

She adjusted the temperature of the shower and shucked off her clothes. She stepped into the tub and drew the shower curtain shut. The hot water felt good. Already she could feel her muscles relaxing. She closed her eyes and enjoyed the lulling warmth of the water.

After several long minutes, the water began to run cold, and she reluctantly opened her eyes. Through the clear plastic of the shower curtain, she could see the steamy mirror on the opposite wall—and a man's face vaguely reflecting from the opaque surface.

With a strangled gasp, Lauren yanked open the curtain. The face was gone.

She twisted off the flow of water and fumbled for a towel as she looked wildly from side to side. Who had it been? Where had he gone?

She wrapped a towel around her and grabbed a pair of scissors out of the vanity drawer. They weren't much of a weapon, but they could inflict a nasty cut or two.

She crept through her bedroom door, thoroughly examining every conceivable hiding place. It was empty, but that didn't necessarily mean the man hadn't run through it and out into the foyer.

Quickly, she flung open the door to the hall. The foyer and stairwell were pitch-black. She listened for sounds of movement. No one could go down the stairs and out the door without making some noise.

When she heard nothing, she edged along the dark foyer to the door of the blue room. Taking a deep breath and raising the scissors in preparation to strike, she thrust open the door.

It, too, was empty.

Silently Lauren crossed the room, looking around the corner, then went back into her own room. No one was there. She had heard no sounds but her own. Experience told her the old floorboards creaked and popped with any footfall, and certainly the steps of a tall man would have been clearly audible, but she had heard nothing.

She sat on her bed and curled her feet up

under her as she looked back into the bathroom. The mirror was still fogged in spots but
was rapidly clearing. From her bed she could
see into the adjoining blue room and its turret
windows and one corner of the bed.

What had she seen? Could it have been no
more than a trick played by the steamy mirror
and clear vinyl shower curtain? Maybe the curtain had a flaw that when viewed under certain
conditions might resemble a face. This seemed
unlikely, but it wasn't impossible.

Would the flaw be such that she would see
dark hair, a stubborn jaw and blue eyes?
Surely no flaw would have a variety of colors in
it. Yet she was positive about the color of his
eyes and hair.

She considered calling the police, but that
meant going down those black stairs and
through the hall with its myriad doors and into
the dark parlor. If she got halfway there and
the lights went out, she knew she would die of
fright on the spot. Besides that, the police
would be certain to say it was all her imagination. That's what they had said during her
junior year in college when she had had that
breakdown, as her mother called it.

She looked around the room again and listened carefully. If a man were in the house,
and if he had heard her showering and come
in to watch, why hadn't he attacked her?
Surely if there was anything to fear from him,
it already would have happened.

Carefully she tried to reconstruct exactly

what had happened. It was no figment of her imagination, because she had been having no fearful thoughts at the time she had seen the reflection. She was, in fact, rather drowsy and completely relaxed. Naturally it had been no dream, because she had been wide-awake and standing in a shower at the time.

She tried to recall the man's features. He was dark, handsome and had incredibly blue eyes. He hadn't looked menacing at all. If anything, his expression was loving and ... wistful. He was the sort of man she would look at twice in a crowd and probably endeavor to meet.

Lauren frowned at the direction her thoughts were taking. This was a prowler, an intruder who had broken into her house and watched her in the shower. She shouldn't logically have romantic thoughts about wanting to meet him or of thinking he was more handsome than Robert, though he had been.

She tried to remember what he had been wearing, but she had only the vague impression of a dark suit and white shirt close about his neck. A burglar in a suit? Ridiculous!

That left only one other possibility, but one that neatly explained his disappearance as well as his clothes. She was haunted, but not by Laura. Her ghost was Nathaniel Padgett himself.

Chapter Eleven

For the next few days, Lauren took baths instead of showers. She left the shower curtain pulled back and locked both doors to the bathroom, but there was no further sign of the mysterious man. Gradually her curiosity overcame her fear. Since her belongings continued to show up in inexplicable places, she had to accept the fact that she did indeed have a ghost. The idea was more frightening in the abstract, she found, than in reality. What would have sounded terrifying, if told to her by a stranger, was more in the nature of intrigue now that it was happening to her personally.

In order to keep her job, Lauren had agreed to an official change in her job status from full-time to part-time. Mr. Combe hadn't cared much for the idea—by this time Mr. Newton had retired and the architectural firm had become Combe and Kinney—but Robert had managed to convince his new partner that the change was best for the company. Robert had done so not only for old time's sake but because he was genuinely worried about Lauren.

This new schedule left Lauren free to spend her afternoons in caring for her house and in planning teas that never quite materialized.

By this time Lauren had discarded most of her modern clothing and wore vintage garments that suggested they might have come from an earlier and more genteel time.

Celia's worries about Lauren increased with every visit. At last she could avoid the subject no longer and came right out with it. "What's happening to you? Why are you changing?"

"Changing?" Lauren stirred her tea and lay the silver spoon in her saucer before lifting the delicate cup to her unrouged lips.

"You know exactly what I mean. You don't wear makeup any more, and you have on long sleeves even though it must be a hundred degrees outside."

"I like this blouse, don't you? Think how long it took someone to hand-stitch all these tucks and ruffles."

"Yes, it's pretty, but it's so old."

"That's the charm of it. With the air-conditioner running, I'm quite comfortable. Aren't you?"

"That's not the point."

"What exactly is the point?"

Celia tried to control her exasperation. "You act as if this were the turn of the century—and I don't mean the one coming up. What's happening to you?"

Lauren purposefully replaced her cup in the saucer. "I've seen him."

"Seen who?"

"The ghost. Nathaniel Padgett." She smiled as though this explained everything.

"Don't give me that. I don't believe in ghosts, and neither do you."

"I do now. I saw him several nights ago. In my shower."

"The ghost was in your shower?" Celia couldn't keep the sarcasm out of her voice.

Lauren laughed. "Not like that. *I* was in the shower. I saw the ghost in the mirror. At first I thought it was a prowler, but of course it wasn't."

Celia wasn't sure what to say. She hadn't expected this. "Maybe you'd better tell me about it."

As she listened to Lauren's account of seeing the blue-eyed man and searching for him, Celia became more alarmed. "You had a prowler. Lauren, you know as well as I do that there are a dozen ways he could have alluded you, especially in that dark foyer. Why, you could have passed right by him."

Lauren shook her head. "I'm telling you it was a ghost. Even at the time, I couldn't see how a prowler could have vanished so silently.

And I'm always careful to keep the outside doors locked."

"Did you search the upper veranda? He might have stepped out there."

"Have you ever in your life heard of a burglar who wore a dark suit and starched white shirt?"

"You must have been mistaken," Celia stubbornly argued.

"Don't you see? That explains why my things move about from time to time." She held up her teaspoon. "I found these in the freezer."

Celia warily eyed the spoon.

"At first I thought it was Laura's ghost—Mrs. Padgett—but now I know it's Nathaniel himself, and he's moving objects about to make contact with me." She smiled and seemed to blush as she lowered her eyes. "I think he's teasing me. It's almost as if he's flirting."

"Now that's ridiculous." Celia stood and paced to the parlor windows. "Lauren, I don't want to alarm you, but I think you were right a while back when you were wondering if someone else has a key to this house."

"I no longer think that."

"Well, I do. Don't you see how that is a more logical explanation for all this? Someone, for some reason, is coming in here and moving your things about. You caught a glimpse of him in your mirror."

"It was Nathaniel."

"Have you ever heard of a ghost with a reflection?" Celia cried out in exasperation.

"How do you know if they do or not?" Lauren countered. "How many have you ever seen?"

"I want you to see a doctor. Please, Lauren!"

"There's nothing wrong with me. Nothing at all."

Celia studied her friend. "You can sit there in your long black skirt, frilly Victorian blouse, and your hair combed into a sort of pompadour and tell me there's nothing wrong with you?"

"Nostalgia is very popular these days. I find I enjoy dressing like this."

"And I guess cucumber sandwiches are also on the rise?"

"I can devil some eggs if you'd prefer that."

"That's not the point." Celia looked toward the hall and regretted what she had to propose. "I think we should search the house."

"Whatever for? You know we're alone here—except, of course, for Nathaniel."

"Stop saying that."

With a sigh Lauren stood and led the way to the stairs. "You're being silly."

"We'll start with the attic." Celia glanced up at the regions above. She didn't want to do this at all.

They searched the attic and found undisturbed dust and spider webs all over everything. In the servant's room, Lauren went to what Celia had assumed was a closet and opened the door to reveal a narrow, dark stairway. Celia drew in a deep breath and tried to quell a wave of claustrophobia.

The stairs led to a closet in the red room and descended past the tiny landing to darkness below. Celia was relieved when Lauren opened the door to the outer room and let in sunlight.

"Don't you have electricity in here?"

"The bulbs are burned out, I think. I never use these stairs, so I haven't replaced them."

"Let's split up. You go toward the green room, and I'll go through your bedroom. Leave all the doors open and we'll meet in the blue room."

"Okay," Lauren said with a smile, "but they won't stay open."

"Yes, they will." Celia opened the door to the foyer and put a vase on the floor to prop it open.

She waited until Lauren went through the end door and opened it wide. Celia could see the length of the green room as far as the shallow L-shaped end. She checked the bathroom and, leaving all the doors wide open, went into the yellow room. Lauren's bedroom was a simpler shape than the others, but since it jutted out over the kitchen, the irregular layout was vaguely disorienting. Celia could never tell which way she was facing in this house.

As before, she left the doors open, using a jar of cold cream to hold the door between the bedrooms. She went in the bathroom and stared at the mirror. It looked perfectly ordinary and, as Lauren had said, her shower curtain was clear plastic with a fat red and yellow tulip design on the lower half. At eye level she would have had an easy view of the mirror.

Celia left the doors open and passed from the yellow room into the blue one. The far-right corner ballooned out into a circular sitting room that filled the turret. The left corner was hidden behind the L-shaped angle.

Celia rounded the corner to see Lauren standing there waiting for her. Lauren's silent stance in the archaic garments made a prickle of fear run up Celia's back. Then Lauren smiled and Celia felt foolish.

"Satisfied?"

Celia nodded. "So far, so good." Her eyes fell on a white garment on the bed. "What's this?"

Lauren's face lit up. "It's my wedding dress. I just finished hemming it last night. Do you like it?"

Celia slowly lifted it. "Wedding dress? You made a wedding dress?"

"That's right. I don't have a sewing machine, so I did it all by hand. But I think that's really the nicest way, don't you?"

Reluctantly Celia raised her eyes. "But you aren't getting married."

"Well, of course I am." Lauren laughed as if her friend had made a joke. "You're to be my maid of honor. Surely you haven't forgotten."

"No, I haven't. I had thought maybe you had."

"That reminds me. I have some more lists to give you. Flowers and names for the guest list, that sort of thing." Lauren vaguely waved her hand. "I looked for your alleged burglar everywhere. There's nobody here but us chickens, as they say."

Celia nodded. The house had no real closets except for the one in Lauren's bedroom, nor was there anything to suggest hidden rooms even though the arrangement of the house was confusing. Besides, this house had been built long after the Civil War and Underground Railroad were memories.

She straightened out the wedding dress on the bed. She couldn't believe Lauren had sewn it and was continuing the delusion that she was going to marry Robert. Celia knew for a fact that he was dating Susan Redlow with some regularity. She could no longer really blame him. Lauren had become very strange indeed.

When they went into the foyer, Celia stopped. All the doors were neatly closed. She opened the nearest one that led to the green room and saw the adjoining doors were also shut. The vase was back in its place on the foyer table. Icy fear crawled up her spine. She jerked her head around to stare at Lauren. Had she tiptoed around and shut them herself?

"See? I told you they won't stay open. Are you ready to search downstairs?"

Celia stayed close to Lauren as they went down. At the hall they split, with Celia going through the formal parlor, library and drawing room. She waited for Lauren in the kitchen.

Her nerves weren't up to the maze of dim pantries.

"See? No burglars." Lauren's eyes were bright as if this were a game that she was thoroughly enjoying. "But I did find this." She held out the jar of cold cream Celia had used to prop open the door of the yellow bedroom. "It was on the dining room table."

Celia recoiled. She knew for a fact the jar had been upstairs only moments before. "You brought it down here," she accused. "When you shut the bedroom doors, you put it in your pocket and brought it downstairs."

Lauren looked confused. "Why would I do a thing like that? And *I* didn't shut those doors. They shut themselves."

Celia headed for the hall. Her purse lay on the table there. "Didn't I leave this in the parlor?"

"I don't know. I didn't notice."

"I have to be going." Panic was building fast, and she felt she had to get away.

"So soon? I haven't given you my new lists."

"Mail them to me. Really, Lauren, I have to go." She fought to keep the panic from her voice.

"All right." Lauren opened the front door, a gracious smile on her face. "It was so nice of you to drop by. Do come again soon."

Celia gave her a peculiar look, but Lauren never let her smile waver. She was a bit embarrassed for Celia that her manners weren't as impeccable as Lauren's own, but then, of course, Celia came from up north somewhere. Lauren was sure that explained it. Girls from Siddel Marsh were taught manners from birth.

Behind her she heard the library door close softly, then that of the drawing room.

Lauren went into the parlor to clear away the tea tray and cups. She caught a glimpse of herself in the mirror and paused. Celia was right about one thing—she really did look like someone from the last turn of the century.

Concern clouded her features. Until recently she had prided herself on wearing only the latest fashions, and she had kept her hair cut in a stylish bob. Why had she decided these clothes and this hair style were more comfortable and more flattering?

She went to the mirror and touched her pale cheek. She wasn't wearing makeup, nor could she recall the last time she had worn any. She looked at the jar of cold cream she still held in her hand. Her fingers tightened on it. Could it be that Laura was possessing her?

The idea was fearful. Possession was a subject fit for lurid horror novels and the whispered ghost stories of children. She had never believed in it. She had never believed in ghosts.

As always when she was upset she went to the window and looked out at the lake. From that angle she could see only a narrow strip of it, but that was enough to calm her. She couldn't see the part where the pier had stood.

Lauren rubbed her temple where the headache lay at bay. She had less memory lapses of late, but the headache rarely left her. At times she seemed to remember things she couldn't possibly know—like the design of the pier and how it had a small summer house at the end, or the appearance of the man who had carved the elaborate "N P L" in the mantel behind her. It was an "L." She was sure of it now. Her initials intertwined forever with Nathaniel's. No, Laura's initials. The ache in her head increased.

She decided to put it out of her mind and clear away the tea things. Lauren had always hated a messy room.

Lauren spent the afternoon polishing silver and refolding the table linens in the sideboard's drawers. Her Aunt Mabel had once told her that a room's neatness depended as much on the parts that were never seen as on the parts that were in plain view.

For supper Lauren made a salad and deviled eggs. Lately she wasn't in the mood to prepare heavy meals. That would come later when she had Robert to care for.

After she washed and dried the few dishes she had dirtied, Lauren went out onto the porch. The night sky was dark with only a pale sliver of moon. Gaudy stars were strewn randomly in the blackness. The lake was so still Lauren imagined she could see the stars' reflections. She sat on the porch rail and leaned against one of the supports. Perhaps Laura had gone to her death on a dark night such as this.

Lauren was convinced the murder had happened at night, but she didn't recall reading that it had.

In the deep shadows, Laura's dress would have looked pale and silvery though it had been yellow, not white, and her hair would have looked darker than it really was. Lauren wondered in a detached way how she knew all this. A man had stood there by the magnolia where the shadows were darkest. Lauren realized with a start that she was *remembering* these things. Her eyes flicked uneasily toward the lighted door of the house. She didn't want to remember.

The man had come out of the darkness then, and Laura had recognized him at once.

Lauren lurched to her feet and backed away from the window and the view of the lake. These weren't her own memories but those of a woman who had been dead 80 years.

She fumbled with the doorknob and let herself into the bright hall. With relief she leaned against the door, shutting out the alien memories.

She closed her eyes and forced herself to conquer her fear. Didn't that prove Laura was possessing her? And to what end? Her murderer must be long dead by now and beyond any justice Lauren might bring about. Or maybe Laura's restless spirit merely wanted someone to know about it and absolve her of the stigma of suicide.

Lauren headed up the stairs. Had Nathaniel

killed his wife? Looking at the facts she knew
from a current viewpoint, Lauren thought it
was likely. After all, she had drowned here at
Four Seasons at a time of the night when only
her husband and their servants were likely to
have been about. Afterward Nathaniel had de-
parted immediately for a long trip to Europe.

From the standpoint of Laura's contemporaries, however, this wasn't all that unusual.
Bereaved spouses often went to extremes of
mourning, sometimes to the extent of leaving
the dead person's belongings untouched or of
permanently stopping a clock the deceased
had owned. Many sought new surroundings in
order to lessen their mourning. Nathaniel had
built this house for his life with Laura, as the
initials in the parlor mantel proved. Perhaps
he had been so heartbroken that he couldn't
face the house and place of her death so soon
after it happened.

Or maybe he had indeed killed her and was
leaving the country before he could be accused.

A low wind moaned in the chimneys. Lauren
hadn't noticed any wind on the porch. In fact
the lake had seemed unnaturally still.

She shivered as she went into her room and
switched on the light. As she always did these
days, Lauren checked the closet and the bathroom before beginning to undress. She did
these things so automatically now that she seldom noticed her actions.

After slipping her voluminous cotton nightgown over her head and buttoning the pearl

buttons to her neck, she put away her clothes and went to turn down the bed. Outside her lace-draped windows was blackness, and she tried not to look at it as she folded back the bedspread. She was afraid more of Laura's memories would appear in her mind.

Nathaniel must have been the killer, she thought as she reached out to pull down the sheet. Again wind moaned in the chimney, and boards popped restlessly in the floor. Who else would have the opportunity to kill her? Women were cosseted in those days and not encouraged to go out alone at night where a stranger might harm them. Had Laura been an heiress? That might supply a motive. Four Seasons would have cost a small fortune to build, even in those days.

Something circled Lauren's wrist, and she froze in the act of drawing down the sheet. The lamp was on, as well as the ceiling light, and she could clearly see nothing was holding her wrist, but she could feel it. It felt like a man's hand.

She jerked back and found no resistance. Nervously she stood erect, rubbing her wrist and looking about. She had felt something similar once before when the lights had gone out. Reflexively she glanced at the oblique view of the bathroom mirror.

After a while she bent over again and pulled down the sheet. This time she felt nothing out of the ordinary. Lauren scowled. Her imagi-

nation was certainly working overtime tonight.

She turned off the ceiling light and lay down.
As part of her nightly ritual, she reached for a
jar of hand cream and scooped out a generous
amount to massage into her hands and arms.
The cream was an expensive brand but one
which was guaranteed to smooth away the
wrinkles and crepe skin Lauren feared and
dreaded.

She wondered if she would ever know the
truth about Laura's death. Laura herself
seemed to think it was important she know.
Once the truth was out, would Laura continue
to possess her? If she told the world Nathaniel
had killed his wife, would she once again be
left in peace?

The wind suddenly struck with such force a
shutter pulled loose and banged frantically
against the house. The lamp beside the bed
blinked twice, then went out.

Lauren jerked bolt upright as she felt the
mattress sag as if someone had sat down beside
her on the bed.

Her scream echoed throughout the suddenly
quiet house. Lauren leaped from the bed and
ran for the door. Someone was in her house!
He had sat beside her on the bed! There was
no way she could be mistaken about that.

She had to escape. Not daring to turn on the
lights, she stumbled down the stairs, grasping
the rail to keep from falling headlong. At the
foot of the stairs she paused to look up, but

there was only darkness there, darkness all around her, pressing in on her, robbing her of her breath.

With strangled sobs Lauren ran toward the front door. As she passed the hall tree, she had the presence of mind to grab her purse. She had to get away, and she had to have car keys to do that.

The front door resisted her efforts to open it, as if something were holding it shut. Lauren cried out again and yanked with all her strength. The door flew open and banged against the wall. Not bothering to shut it, she ran out into the night.

Grass and pebbles were sharp against her bare feet, and her nightgown billowed as she ran. She avoided the lake side and circled around to the garage. The drive's gravel cut into her feet; the garage was menacingly black. Lauren didn't dare stop.

She felt her way down the side of her car and forced open the driver's door. Tears were blinding her as she dumped her purse out onto the seat in search of her keys. All the horror stories she had ever seen or heard were forcing her into a state of hysteria.

Finally she found the right key and thrust it into the ignition. On the second try the engine started. With a squeal of tires she backed out and looked fearfully up at her house as she tried to find the right gear to send the car forward.

The light was on in her room, and from here

the house looked peaceful enough, though she knew better. As she sped around the corner and toward the street, she noticed the front door was shut.

Sobbing, she drove as fast as she dared down the quiet streets. Within minutes she pulled into Robert's driveway. She stopped the car with such force it bounced on its shocks. Lauren was out of the car, running for the house before the car had stopped rocking.

"Robert!" she screamed as she poked the doorbell and pounded on the door. "Robert! Let me in!"

She heard the sound of scurrying feet, and when Robert opened the door, she fell sobbing into his arms.

"Lauren! What are you doing here? What's wrong?"

"I...someone..." She could find no words to tell him what had frightened her. "Someone is in my house."

"What? Someone broke in?" He drew her into the house and flipped on the light. He looked as if he had been sound asleep. "Have you called the police?"

"No, no! I didn't hear anyone break in. I was awake, and someone sat on the edge of my bed." She stared up at him, her eyes full of horror.

Robert looked down at her. "Say that again?"

"I'm telling you someone sat on my bed. I was turning down the covers and listening to the storm and someone, something, grabbed my wrist."

"What storm?"

"I couldn't see anything, so I tried to tell myself I was imagining it. Then I lay down and the lights flickered and went off—and somebody sat on the side of my bed."

Robert stood gazing down at her. She saw pity in his eyes.

"Don't look at me that way. It's true!"

"I never said it wasn't." He reached past her to open the front door. "Look. There's no storm."

"But there was. I heard the wind moaning in the chimney like it did when that hurricane blew through. Remember?" She waited until he nodded. "It was blowing so hard a shutter was banging against the house."

"Lauren, those shutters are merely decorative. They're screwed to the walls and couldn't possibly bang on anything. If one came loose, it would drop to the ground."

She doubled her fist and hit his arm as hard as she could. "Damn it, Robert, I heard it!"

"Okay, okay." He rubbed his arm and glared back at her. "So you can stay here tonight. Is that what you want?"

Lauren paused, then nodded. She couldn't go back to Four Seasons—not while those shutters were banging and someone was sitting on her bed and the whole house was filled with Laura's memories.

As she followed Robert down the hall, she

said miserably, "Do you believe in possession—by a dead person, I mean?"

"Not in a million years," he gruffly replied.

"Robert, I think Laura is possessing me."

"Bullshit." He pushed open the door to his guest room.

"In here?" She had assumed she would sleep in his room with him.

"Take it or leave it."

Lauren went in and gazed down at the sterile double bed in the dull little room. "Thank you, Robert," she said over her shoulder.

"Don't mention it."

He shut the door behind her, and she looked around. Beige carpet, off-white walls, beige curtains, furniture that could have come from any inexpensive furniture store. This was the house Robert had imagined she would move into after their marriage. Why, it was as dull as Robert himself.

She went to the bed and pulled down the covers. As she lay down, she noticed the bed had the faint smell of linens that needed airing.

She left the light on and stared up at the white ceiling with its plain white light fixture. Up until now, she hadn't noticed just how dull Robert was. A real lover would have at least invited her to share his bed. A courageous man would have taken her back home and proved to her the house was safe and would have then taken her to bed.

"I've a mind not to marry him at all," she whispered in spite. That made her feel better.

Robert Kinney wasn't her only suitor. She was young yet. She could still have her pick.

Lauren closed her eyes and prepared to wait for morning. She wanted to be gone before Robert awoke.

Chapter Twelve

Lauren left Robert's house in the early dawn. For a few moments she considered leaving Robert a note but decided against it. There was really nothing to say that could be put in a note. She couldn't explain that she was leaving because she wanted a lover who was man enough to take her into his own bed and to fight dragons for her, instead of merely offering her a place to sleep in the spare room. She didn't know how to say she needed someone who would believe what she said when her fears seemed unbelievable even to herself. No note she could possibly write would change Robert into someone else.

She was embarrassed to drive home in her nightgown with her hair wild all over her head, but she had no choice. She avoided the main streets, however, and met few cars.

At her house she slowed to a stop out front and studied the massive structure. Dawn was pink on the eastern window glass, and all the shutters were properly in place just as Robert had said they would be. In the light of day, she realized she couldn't possibly have heard one banging when they weren't made to shut at all. The front door was securely closed, and there were no tree limbs blown about the yard. For all external appearances, the commotion of the night before might never have happened at all.

Lauren drove around back and parked in one of the wide spaces in the garage. In the dim light, she stuffed all her belongings back into her purse and got out of the car. Her feet were bruised and tender from her flight, and she hobbled painfully onto the grass.

At the base of the porch steps she paused. What would she find inside? Utter chaos? Laura's restless spirit?

More than mildly apprehensive, she climbed the steps and unlocked the back door. Pushing it open, she hesitated. It tapped gently against the wall. There was no other sound.

Lauren stepped in and looked about, fearful of what she might find, but nothing was disturbed or out of place. Pale sunlight slanting through a window made a rectangle on her kitchen floor. The house smelled of lemon oil and cloves as it always did.

She put her purse on the kitchen table and tiptoed through the pantries to the dining room. The house was still, and outside she could hear the early stirring of birds.

In the hall she stood for several long minutes, staring up the stairs. The grandfather clock on the landing rhythmically ticked as it must have for decades. The upstairs foyer was dim, but no more so than ever. The stairs to the attic were darker still, but not threateningly so.

Rather than going upstairs, she completed the circuit of the downstairs rooms and ended in the drawing room. She had slept very little during the night and was exhausted, physically as well as mentally. Whatever was happening to her, she thought, would simply have to happen. She was too tired to fight.

Her eyes went to the Ouija board, and for several minutes she stared at it as if she were transfixed. Then she picked it up and settled into one of the wing-backed chairs, resting the board on her lap. With careful deliberation, she put her fingers on the planchette. "Laura?" she said.

The planchette quivered, then in a graceful curve, went to the word "No."

Lauren closed her eyes and tried to concentrate. "I want to speak to Laura."

The pointer circled the board and hovered again at "No." Before she could speak again, it began to arc across the letters. It spelled out, "You are Laura."

"No!" Lauren gasped, tears choking her voice. "I'm Lauren Hamilton."

"You were Laura," the planchette explained as it moved in gentle swirls as if not to frighten her. Then it indicated March 10th—the day of Laura's death, the day of Lauren's birth.

Lauren took her fingers from the board as she mulled over this suggestion. She had, of course, heard of reincarnation, though she wasn't at all sure she believed in it, but she had to know what was going on. Swallowing the lump in her throat, she put her fingers back on the triangle of wood. "Are you Nathaniel Padgett?"

The planchette glided under her fingers to the "Yes." Fear began to rise in her in spite of the board's gentle movements.

"Did you kill Laura?" she whispered.

The pointer went to "No" with such force it almost fell from the board.

"Then who did?"

It began to swing in wild arcs and finally clattered to the floor. Lauren's wide eyes stared down at it. This time she knew the planchette had not been maneuvered by Celia or Susan, and her subconscious couldn't be at blame, because the answers had not been the ones she had expected.

She was Laura, reincarnated. Somehow the idea wasn't all that surprising to her. If anything it was a relief. Laura wasn't possessing her—she *was* Laura.

And she had been right about the cause of

Laura's death being murder and not suicide or accidental drowning, but Nathaniel himself didn't know who murdered her. She had felt his distress all the way up her hands and arms. Perhaps that was why he was still in the house.

She bent and picked up the planchette. "Are you here because you can't find peace until you learn who murdered her?" Lauren found she still had to speak of Laura as a separate entity.

"No," it indicated. "I love you."

As Lauren stared in shock, it began to spell "Love" again. She took her fingers away.

Nathaniel wasn't there to avenge but rather to protect. She recalled the repaired lock, the watered plants, and several other small things she assumed she had done herself but forgotten. Nathaniel was there for her.

After several minutes she put the Ouija board away and went upstairs. She was tired, so tired she could hardly think.

Her bed was turned down just as she had left it the night before. Lauren dragged herself into it and was asleep before her muscles had time to relax.

The faint sound of her telephone ringing, far below her, awoke Lauren from a deep sleep. She opened her eyes, blinked, then closed them again. She had forgotten to go to work. No doubt that would be Robert calling to complain, and she didn't want to go through that again.

After a while the ringing stopped, and Lauren rolled on to her back. Something on the covers rustled. She opened her eyes to see flowers—roses, begonias, sweet william, all the flowers that bloomed in Four Seasons's gardens—strewn over her coverlet.

Amazed, Lauren sat up and lifted a rose to gaze at it. Across the room she saw words written on her dresser mirror in lipstick. "Don't be afraid of me," it said.

She leaned back against the headboard and gathered an armload of flowers to her breast. How could she possibly be afraid of someone who covered her bed in flowers? She smiled the secret smile of a woman who is falling in love.

All day she refused to answer her phone. Late that afternoon she heard a knocking on her door and saw Robert's shape through the etched glass, but she refused to answer it. Let it be on his conscious, she thought vengefully, that he hadn't been man enough to keep her.

As Robert went away Lauren hummed "In the Good Old Summertime." She couldn't quite remember all the words yet, but they were gradually coming back to her. Soon, she knew, her memories of Laura would be complete. One name, Frank, kept echoing in the corners of her mind, but she wasn't at all sure who he was or why his name would be important to her. A brother perhaps? Or maybe one of Laura's discarded suitors? Laura had been popular—Lauren was certain of that. She could remember being sought after by many young men, but she had chosen Nathaniel.

She cleaned the house as thoroughly as if she were expecting company, and as she worked she was aware of almost inaudible sounds, sounds that might once have frightened her before she had begun to understand. They seemed to be fragments of words as if someone were speaking from far away, but she couldn't hear them perfectly enough to make out any of the words.

But soon she would hear him perfectly. She was sure of it.

For supper Lauren ate cheese and crackers and drank a glass of wine. On hot summer days such as this one she hated to cook. She ate on the porch where a breeze so often stirred from the lake. Behind her the windows were open, and the curtains shifted prettily in the breeze. Around the corner of the house she heard the constant hum of the air-conditioner's motor, but she ignored it. The air-conditioner, like Robert, was part of something she was leaving behind.

After she finished eating, she scattered the crumbs into the yard for the birds and went inside. She had only her wine glass and the cheese knife to wash. As she let water run in the sink, she studied her reflection in the blade of the knife. Still young. Young and pretty.

Condensation dripping in the well drew her attention as she finished washing the knife. With her new understanding, Lauren looked over at the well. Now she knew this fear of the well had been one of her first memories from Laura's life. Lauren had no reason to fear wells, but Laura did. As a child Laura had seen her father and his hired hands fish the body of a tramp from a well. Her mother had made her watch in order to instill a fear that would keep young Laura from playing near one and perhaps falling to her own death. The lesson had worked too well, however, and Laura had been deathly afraid of falling into a well, so afraid that the fear had lasted all her life and beyond.

Lauren put away the knife and wine glass and went upstairs. All around her she heard the gentle murmur of words not quite comprehensible. Instead of going into her own room, she went to the door of the Winter room.

The wedding dress lay on the bed, as pale as a promise. Lauren picked it up and held it against her. Now that she knew Robert for the cad he was, the wedding was out of the question. She wondered how to tell him so without breaking his heart. And there was Celia as well. Celia would be disappointed at not being maid of honor. Lauren smiled fondly. Celia, like Robert, would just have to understand.

Lauren found a hanger in her closet and took it back to the blue room. This dress was too special to hang among the ones she wore every day. By running her palm over the wall, she found the nail where Laura had hung her gowns. The wedding dress looked startlingly white against the dark blue pattern of the wall-paper.

She went to the rounded windows and looked out at the lake. There was no moon that night, and in the blackness she could almost imagine that the pier was still there, that she was still Laura Padgett and that Nathaniel would step into the room at any moment.

Lauren undressed and lay down on the sleigh bed, pulling the sides of the snowflake quilt up over her.

In the doorway to the foyer, the darkness seemed to gather to itself in front of the dark paneled door. A vague shape began to form, the shape of a man she had once loved with all her heart.

Lauren watched so intently that her eyes ached, but the form dissolved, leaving only the crosspiece of the paneling to suggest broad shoulders and the upright to hint at the shape of a head.

Not yet, she realized with a sigh of disappointment, not yet. But soon.

Lauren dug through her closet, pulling out all her modern clothes. Since she no longer wore them at all, they only took up space. She folded them carefully and put them in paper grocery bags. She looked wonderingly at what had been her favorite pair of jeans. Now she couldn't imagine wanting to wear them, especially not in public. They were bordering on scandalous the way they hugged her body and separated her legs. She liked her new clothes much better.

She carried the bags down and put them in the back of her car. Her new lifestyle was so enjoyable, the best of two worlds, really. She could enjoy the modern conveniences of automobile transportation and still have the simpler pursuits of needlework and charcoal sketching. She found she had been rather talented in her life as Laura and had drawn Nathaniel from memory. In her recollection, of course, he was young since she had died so soon after their wedding. She wondered if he had aged well. There were no photographs of him that she had been able to find.

She drove to Celia's apartment and knocked on her door. When Celia opened it, Lauren greeted her with a smile and the first of the bags.

"What's this?"

"I've been cleaning out my closet," Lauren explained, "and I thought you might like to have some things. I have several more bags in the car. Will you help me bring them up?"

Celia looked mystified, but she obligingly helped Lauren make two trips to carry up all the bags. "Now will you tell me what all this is?"

"Clothes, of course. Clothes I no longer use. We are about the same size, and I thought you might want them."

Celia pulled a red dress out of the nearest

bag. "This is your new dress. Why, you've only worn it once or twice."

"I know, but the color is so ... red, and I don't feel comfortable in such a short skirt." Lauren knelt and pulled out a bathing suit. "I know you'll like this. I've never used it at all. See? The tags are still on it."

"I can't accept these." Celia sat on the floor beside Lauren. "I can't take all your clothes."

"This isn't all of them, silly. I kept quite a few things."

"Lauren ..."

"Actually these are to ease your disappointment in what I must tell you, not because I thought you needed them. Please don't be offended."

"I'm not offended, just surprised. What disappointment?"

"I've decided not to marry Robert."

Celia stared at her. "Oh?"

Lauren averted her eyes. "Something happened the other night, something very important, but I misunderstood and ran away. Now I see I was being ridiculous, but that was before I fully understood. Anyway, I ran to Robert, naturally expecting him to act as my protector."

"Protector against what?"

"Nathaniel, of all things. See? I told you it was ridiculous."

Celia made no comment.

Lauren blushed a bit as she confided, "I expected Robert to let me stay overnight at his house—which he did, but I expected him to offer me his bed." She blushed more deeply. "Please don't be shocked or think wrong of me, but we have in the past, well, shared intimacies."

"I should hope so."

"But instead he put me in the guest room, a horrid little box of a room that was the color of oatmeal. That's when I realized Robert is dull."

"I know he is, but you must have noticed that before now. We've discussed him not being a thrill a minute, but you always said you liked his stability."

"I was wrong. He has no more imagination than a bean. Even after I told him what happened, he couldn't understand and expressed no sympathy."

"Try me. Tell me all about it."

Lauren shyly laughed. "I was upstairs in my bedroom and someone touched me—on my wrist. At first I was startled, of course, but I went to bed anyway. It was quite late. Then all at once the lights began to act funny like they do sometimes."

"You've got to have someone out to check the wiring. It must be dangerous."

"And someone sat on the side of my bed."

"I beg your pardon?"

"On my bed! Nathaniel sat on the edge of my bed. Of course at the time I didn't know it was him, and I ran away to Robert's house."

"You actually saw someone?"

"No, the lights were out. I almost saw him last night, but he couldn't quite materialize. I frequently hear his voice now—not the words, exactly, but just his voice."

"Lauren, you're frightening me. We have to do something about this. You need help."

"No, no, don't you see? It's only Nathaniel. There's no reason for me to be afraid of him."

Celia could only stare at her.

"And there's more," Lauren said, her eyes shining with excitement.

"More?"

"I'm Laura."

"Look, I think—"

"Oh, I know I'm Lauren Hamilton, but I was also Laura Padgett."

"You think Laura is possessing you?" Celia sounded disbelieving.

"I did at first, and that's one reason I was afraid. Now I know I used to *be* Laura. Don't you see? I was afraid of being my real self." Lauren laughed and covered her mouth coquettishly. "I was afraid of me."

"I think you're going to have to explain that. I'm not following you."

"Laura died on March 10th, 1910. Forty-five years later I was born on March 10th."

"It's only a coincidence."

"You can see how similar our names are, and we both lived at Four Seasons. I know, you're going to say those are coincidences, too, but lately I've begun to have her memories. I know why I became so afraid of the well in my

231

kitchen. Laura was terrified of wells because of something that happened in her childhood. *Hers*, not mine. I recall what flowers were planted in the gardens and where the pier stood. It had a little summer house at the end. I guess Nathaniel had it torn down after I—Laura—died. The blue snowflake quilt is very similar to one Laura—I—made for the sleigh bed."

"I don't understand any of this." Celia got to her feet and went into her kitchenette. "Do you want some coffee?"

"No, thank you." Lauren got off the floor and sat on a chair, spreading her full skirt over her knees. "It's reincarnation. You're always reading about children in India who recall their former families or child prodigies who never have to be taught to play the piano. This is no different."

"Yes, it is. This is weird." Celia came back with a steaming coffee cup and sat on the couch opposite Lauren.

"I don't know why I'm remembering my past life, but I am. I've gone to the library and looked up people and landmarks Laura knew and I've been right every time. *Every* time." She smiled shyly. "Nathaniel is waiting for me."

"No way! I found the chink in all this. Laura and Nathaniel are both dead. He has no reason to wait for you."

"But *I'm* Laura. I was reborn before Nathaniel died. Maybe I came back in search of him. Isn't it romantic?"

"It's spooky. Lauren, have you listened to how this all sounds?"

Lauren nodded. "I know it's incredible. I fought against believing it for ever so long. It makes sense though. I know for a fact Nathaniel is still in the house. He was the face I saw in the mirror that night." She demurely lowered her eyes. "He's killingly handsome."

"Hear how you talk? You move like a stranger and have started dressing like, well, I don't know what."

"I can see you're confused," Lauren said with kindness in her voice. "Believe me. I understand."

Celia sighed. "So what next? What are you going to do about all this?"

Lauren's eyes became troubled. "I don't know. I feel I have to remember who killed Laura, but so far that's unclear. I suppose the trauma wiped out the memory." She frowned as she looked across at her friend. "I suppose I should be concerned about it, but I find I much prefer Laura's life to my own."

Chapter Thirteen

Lauren dialed the telephone and held it gingerly to her ear. Lately the modern conveniences seemed more and more alien to her. "Robert? This is Lauren." She knew he would recognize her voice, but she wanted to do this exactly right. "I think you should come over here. There's something I must tell you."

She waited patiently while he roared at her over the phone line. "Yes, I know you're at work. I called you, remember? No, I can't discuss it over the phone. Tell Mr. Combe something important has come up, and you have to be gone for a while." Not waiting for him to go into all the reasons he couldn't or wouldn't come, she hung up. She knew he would soon be on his way to her.

Going into the hall, she put on her wide-brimmed straw hat and tied it under her chin. She had some gardening to do and didn't want to spoil her skin with freckles. "I'm going out to the garden," she called up the empty staircase. "I'll not be out long."

The half-heard murmur drifted back to her. In the last few days, she had begun to talk to Nathaniel, and he seemed to answer her. She felt secure knowing he was there, just out of sight.

She took her gardening gloves and slipped them on as she went outside. It was a lovely day for gardening. White clouds piled in masses like whipped cream just beyond the lake, but overhead the sky was clear. By evening there might be rain, but that was hours away.

She had started a small garden down by the lake where Laura had planned one so long ago. The garden was to have bordered the shallow steps up to the pier and was modeled after a knot garden Laura and Nathaniel had admired on their honeymoon in England. Lauren had had some difficulty finding exactly the right plants, but she was pleased with the result.

A car full of teenagers honked as they were passing by and shouted something at her, but Lauren ignored them. Children these days were taught no manners at all. Whenever she went somewhere, people stared at her and whispered among themselves. She always tried to pretend not to notice. They might be rude, but Lauren had had an impeccable up-bringing.

At the garden she knelt on the grass and be-gan pulling weeds. The plants had only been in the ground a few days, but already the weeds were trying to take over. Lauren couldn't help comparing them to the rude people she en-countered in town. If something wasn't done about them soon, they—like weeds—would overrun everything.

Robert's car pulled into her drive. Lauren pretended not to notice. This was going to be an unpleasant discussion, and she wasn't eager to get into it. She heard his car door slam and the sound of his footsteps crossing the grass. The sound touched an illusive memory, and Lauren straightened in her effort to recall it.

"Well?" Robert demanded abruptly. "I as-sume you have a good reason for making me come out here?"

"Yes, I do." Lauren stood and began to pull off her gloves. "Let's sit on the porch where it's shady."

"I'm not going to be here that long."

She led the way to the porch, as if he hadn't spoken. This had to be handled exactly right. She wished she could discuss it properly with Nathaniel. One-sided conversations were so unsatisfying.

After taking a seat in one of the rattan chairs she said, "I'm not going to work any longer."

"What? Not work? How do you expect to make ends meet?" he demanded.

"I have a bit of money put by, and I shall live on the interest."

"You couldn't possibly have enough money in the bank for that," he bluntly countered. "I know what a large down payment you put on this house, and all these repairs and this redecorating have cost you a bundle."

Lauren looked at him in some surprise. Had she confided all that to him? She had no recollection of it. "I'll get by."

"Actually, it saves me having to fire you. Combe told me last week your employment would have to be terminated. I've been trying to avoid telling you—for old times' sake."

"Auld lang syne," she said with a smile. "We did have some nice times together, didn't we?" She sighed and added, "Those are over, however. Robert, I can't marry you."

He stared at her.

"You can see now why I had to see you in person. Some things must be done face to face. Unfortunately this is one of them. I hope I haven't hurt you too deeply."

"Damn it, Lauren, we don't—"

"Please don't curse. I find it offensive." She favored him with a serene smile. "I'd rather not go into my reasons for disappointing you. They're rather personal."

Robert sat on the edge of his chair and leaned forward, resting his elbows on his knees. "I don't know what to say to you."

"There's nothing to say, really. I hope in time you can find someone who will make you

237

happy. I would like to think you and I are still friends."

"Don't dump all this on me and then say you want to be my friend. That's the worst thing a woman can say to a man when they break up. Of course," he added, "we aren't all that close anymore, but still . . ."

"Whatever you say, Robert. Make it easy on yourself."

"This isn't easy on me. I feel guilty about you."

"Guilty? Why?"

"Look at you!" He stabbed a finger toward her gardening hat. "You look like something from another century."

Lauren stood up and went down the porch steps as she replaced her gloves. "There's no reason to be derogatory. I've tried to let you down gently. The least you could do is be a gentleman about it." The nagging headache was beginning behind her eyes, and the brilliant sunlight on the lake didn't help any.

"Don't walk away from me," he called out as he started after her. "I should have said this long before, but now I'm going to tell you."

The threat seemed to echo in her pounding head. Lauren touched her temples with the back of her wrist. She didn't want to hear Robert's threats.

"There's something wrong with you," he snapped as he caught up with her.

"A headache," she murmured, "only a headache."

He appeared not to hear her. "I think you're losing your grip on reality. Hell, I *know* you are. For months you've talked about us getting married, even though I've told you as tactfully as possible that I'm not ready to take that step. Celia says you've even made a wedding dress. She's as worried about you as I am."

Lauren blinked. The sunlight was much too bright. The glare off the lake was blinding.

"I've written your mother and told her what's going on with you," Robert continued. "She called me last night and told me what happened to you in college. Why didn't you tell me you'd been hospitalized?"

"She always calls it my breakdown, as if I were an automobile or a lawn mower."

"She told me about your Aunt Mabel, too. You never mentioned having an aunt in a mental ward."

The headache was increasing in its fierceness. Lauren felt as if her brain was about to burst.

"You need help. Do you hear me? Look at me!"

Lauren felt his hands pull her roughly about. Her eyes, dazed by the glare off the water, were half-blinded. She could see only his silhouette and dim features. She recoiled instantly. "Frank! Frank Burleson!"

"What? What did you say?"

"Frank Burleson, my gardener."

"I don't know what the hell my grandfather

has to do with this. What are you raving about now?"

Lauren's eyes were wide with panic. She remembered! With a strangled scream she jerked away from Robert and, lifting her long skirts, ran for the house.

"You're sick. Do you hear me? Sick!" Robert shouted after her.

Lauren ran faster. She slammed into the house and frantically twisted the lock shut. She had dropped her gloves and her hat had blown off her head, but she couldn't go after them. She drew the curtains aside and watched Robert go to his car and drive away. He would be back, she knew with a deep dread. Now that he knew she remembered, he would be back.

Frank Burleson! Why hadn't she remembered that Robert's mother was a Burleson? Why hadn't that dreadful name sparked a memory?

The house was absolutely silent as she went from door to door securing the locks. When she was positive no one could get in, she sank down in the winged-back chair in the drawing room.

The terrible memories wouldn't stop. She remembered Frank Burleson as she had known him in his youth. He had been handsome in a rough sort of way. She had been attracted by his brawny, sunburned arms and wind-tangled hair. He had been so different from Nathaniel, who was a gentleman at all times.

Laura had been a flirt, and she was used to

men who knew how to play her teasing games. Frank hadn't. He had taken her all too seriously. One day while Nathaniel was in town, Frank had found her in the hothouse that had stood behind the carriage house, and he had had his way with her.

Laura was hurt and frightened half out of her wits. Rape was a crime that was only whispered about and then only in the vaguest of terms, but there was nothing vague about what Frank had done to her.

She hadn't dared tell Nathaniel. Not only would he have killed Frank, but everyone in town would have known of her shame. Laura had become withdrawn and had poured all her nervous energy into various good causes.

Frank, when he didn't get fired or shot, assumed Laura had enjoyed it. He had actually told her so. She had denied it with all her might, but he had only laughed. In time, he said, Nathaniel would leave her alone again, and she would be his for the taking.

Not knowing what else to do, Laura began to buy her safety. All the extra money she could glean out of her household expenses went into Frank's pocket, but it was never enough. Nathaniel, who was jealous by nature, began to be suspicious. He accused her of having a lover in town. Naturally Laura denied it, but she couldn't prove her innocence.

At last she had reached the end of her endurance. Nathaniel was heartbroken over his doubts of her faithfulness; Frank had decided the money alone wasn't enough. He wanted her body as well, or he threatened to tell Nathaniel she had propositioned him. In Nathaniel's state of mind, Laura had thought he might believe Frank.

She told Frank to meet her at midnight on the pier. After Nathaniel was asleep, she took out all the ready cash from their safe.

As she stepped out to the end of the pier, Frank came out of the summerhouse. Laura told him it was all over. He could take the money and disappear, or she would tell Nathaniel about the rape and blackmail. Frank became angry, and they argued.

Laura turned to run back to the house, but he struck her from behind. The blow hit her between the shoulder blades, knocking the wind from her lungs. As she struggled to get her breath to scream, Frank threw her into the water.

Laura knew how to swim, at least well enough to reach shore, but Frank jumped in and grabbed her skirts, pulling her under the water. Laura had fought, but each time she tried to scream her mouth filled with water and finally so did her lungs.

She had a vague memory of floating over herself as her body sank limply under the water, of Frank looking about with furtive, animal-like eyes and running away in the darkness.

After that she had no memory at all until she was Lauren Hamilton at her fifth birthday party.

Lauren had tears flowing down her cheeks, but she didn't remember when she had started to cry. Robert was Frank's grandson. There was a strong family resemblance between them. Maybe that was what had attracted her to him in the first place. His grandfather was long dead. No one had ever suspected Frank as Laura's killer because no one knew he had a motive. Frank was smart. He hadn't missed a single day of work, because one newspaper account mentioned him as being on hand when Laura's body was discovered. He had helped Nathaniel pull her out of the water.

She felt sick at her stomach. For years she had dated Robert and planned to marry him. She had even been his lover. The idea left her nauseated.

There was a frantic pounding on her front door. Lauren turned her dull eyes toward the hall. She could hear Celia calling out her name. Over and over Celia shouted and pounded at the door, but Lauren didn't move. There was no reason to talk to her. Robert had obviously filled her with his lies—lies about her being insane.

Celia tried all the doors. Laura could hear her on the porch, peering in the windows and calling Lauren's name. The large chair hid her, however, and the room was dark and sheltering. No one could see her. No one could get in.

Celia's voice broke as if she were crying, but Lauren remained still. She didn't want to hear about hospitals and how everyone was doing what was best for her. She had heard all that before during her college years—during her breakdown. "Like an automobile or a lawn mower," she had said. Lauren smiled. Robert, as usual, hadn't seen the humor in that. Humans didn't break down. Lauren was tired of hearing people say that she did.

After a while, Celia gave up and went away. Lauren sighed with relief. Her nerves were frayed from the constant banging and shouting.

She looked back at the windows. Dusk was falling. She had lost hours again, but this time she didn't care. That no longer had any relevance to her. Thunder rolled over the lake as Lauren got out of the chair. She went to rest her fingertips briefly on the Ouija board. It had proved to be a friend, after all. It had brought her back in contact with Nathaniel.

Moving like someone in a dream, Lauren went into the hall and up the broad staircase. Her hand ran up the smooth rail one last time. Endings and beginnings, she thought. That's what it was all about.

She went into the blue room and began to undress, her eyes never wavering from the wedding dress that hung on the wall. In the fitful light of sunset and lightning flashes, the dress seemed to glow with a brilliance of its own.

After putting on her prettiest underwear, Lauren slipped the wedding dress over her head. It settled on her body in luxurious folds, molding her hips and breasts and arms. Lauren fastened the dozens of white satin buttons on the bodice and at the wrists.

The storm was moving closer. It was almost over the lake. She patted her hair to be sure it was in place. She wanted to look her best for this.

Not bothering to turn on the lights, Lauren went back downstairs, her white dress seeming wraithlike in the gloom.

At the door she paused and looked back over her shoulder. The house was perfectly quiet as if it were listening and watching.

"I love you," she said softly. The words seemed to murmur into the corridor and dark corners and up the black stairwell.

Lauren smiled because she knew he had heard her. She opened the door and drew in a deep breath of the heavy air. The rain hadn't started yet, but when it did it would come down in torrents.

As she crossed the lawn, lightning limned the woods and lake, followed closely by crashing thunder. Lauren didn't flinch. Such things held no fear for her anymore.

She went to where the pier had stood and looked down at her new garden. Someone else would have to take care of it, she supposed. She had more important things to do.

She waded out into the water. It was colder than she had expected. It tugged at her satin and lace skirts and made them float about her. As she waded deeper, Lauren pressed the skirt underwater. Her movements were calm and patient. She knew exactly what to do.

She was chest-deep when the bottom dropped off sharply. For just an instant she felt panic and confusion. Why was she out here?

A burst of lightning made her squint, and she turned to see the house. Four Seasons stood there as solid and protecting as always. It had always been her haven.

As she watched, the lightning washed over it again, and she clearly saw a man silhouetted in the upper window of the turret. Nathaniel.

She back-paddled out farther as she watched the window. Under his gaze she felt calm and reassured.

As the rain slicked over the water, Lauren let her head sink beneath it.

Epilogue

Celia helped Mrs. Hamilton pack Lauren's belongings. Robert came over to help with the boxes and furniture, as did Mark. Some of the larger pieces like the sideboard in the dining room and the sleigh bed in the Winter bedroom were too large to fit through the doorways, so Mrs. Hamilton said they could be sold with the house.

"What about that grandfather clock on the landing?" Celia asked.

"It never worked," Robert brusquely said.

"Are you sure? I thought it did." She looked at it for a moment, trying to remember if she had heard it strike or if Lauren had only told her it had. She couldn't recall.

Robert stood at the foot of the stairs frowning up at the foyer above. "We had a fight, you know," he said in a low voice so Mrs. Hamilton wouldn't hear.

"Yes, I know. You told me."

A muscle tensed in his jaw. "How was I to know it would push her to suicide?"

"It wasn't your fault. We all knew she was sick."

"The last words we exchanged were words of anger. I can't stop thinking about that." He turned his tortured eyes toward Celia. "She was wearing a wedding dress when they pulled her out."

"I know. I was there, remember?"

"Oh, that's right. I forgot. My mind has been all mixed up these past few days."

"That's certainly understandable. I'm not thinking too clearly myself." She followed his gaze up the stairs. "When you told me about your argument I came out here to see about her, but she wouldn't let me in. I thought I saw her sitting in one of those big chairs in the drawing room, but I couldn't be sure. The room was dark, and there was a glare on the glass. Robert, do you think I could have prevented it if I had forced my way in?"

"I don't know."

"I've thought about it over and over. If I hadn't left to get you, if I had kicked open a door or broken out a window, Lauren might still be alive."

He drew in a deep breath and let it out slowly. "You probably couldn't have stopped her. For all we know she was already in the water. The coroner said he wasn't sure of the exact time of death." He rubbed his eyes as if he hadn't slept in days. "A wedding dress. I just can't get over that. If that wasn't a slam at me, I don't know what was."

"You said she told you she wouldn't marry you. Remember telling me that?"

"I know, but what else could it mean? Maybe she was trying to force me into setting a date. I don't know. And then she called me by my grandfather's name. I can't figure it out."

"I guess we never will."

"What happened to the wedding dress?"

"Mrs. Hamilton asked me to get rid of it. She couldn't bear to see it again."

A soft sound almost like a muffled laugh came floating down the stairs. "Did you hear that?" Celia asked.

"Hear what?"

"Never mind." She frowned as she looked at the closed bedroom doors.

"I have to help Mrs. Hamilton finish packing," Robert said. "All this physical exertion seems to help me."

Celia nodded as she started up the stairs. "I'll check one last time upstairs."

She didn't want to go up there. The house had always given her the creeps. She had seen Lauren pulled out of the lake and buried in Siddel Marsh's old cemetery. She knew Lauren couldn't possibly be up there. Yet she knew

Lauren's laugh, and even as she climbed past the landing she heard it again.

The foyer was dim, and Celia felt a prickle of nerves as she pushed open the door of the yellow room. It was, of course, empty. Without Lauren's furniture and clothes and keepsakes the room was as bare and derelict as it must have been when Lauren first saw it. The paper was splotched with medallions the color of dried mustard and was working loose at the ceiling and corners. The yellow-brown designs in the carpet were worn to the backing in spots. Celia could feel no trace of Lauren in this room.

She walked through to the Winter room and paused to look down at the great sleigh bed. The quilt of blue snowflakes lay folded neatly across its foot.

Odd, Celia thought. She could have sworn she had packed that. She picked it up and went to the turret window. The rain had stopped, and blue sky was reflected in the sparkling water. Her eyes lowered to the place where someone had seen a panel of white cloth floating beneath the water. Even when they pulled her out and lay her body on the muddy bank, even when they buried her, Celia couldn't believe it. She kept thinking this was all a fantastic misunderstanding and that Lauren would step through the door at any minute.

Celia could almost hear her laughing.

She turned back to the room and looked at the bare mattress of the sleigh bed. It was one of the old feather ones and too moldy for resale.

Clearly imprinted on its surface were two in-
dentations.

Impossible, Celia thought. No one had lain
on that bed. Probably it hadn't been used since
Old Man Padgett died in it. Again the almost
inaudible sound drifted through the room.

Celia looked about sharply. "Lauren?" she
whispered, then realized that was impossible.

All the same, Celia lay the folded quilt back
on the foot of the bed and backed toward the
door. The air in the room seemed thicker somehow, and Celia wasn't sure she wanted to stay
around to see what might happen next.

After all of Lauren Hamilton's belongings
were taken away, the house went on the market. At first there were many eager to look at
it—not to buy it, but merely to look. Then the
firehouse itself caught on fire, the organist at
one church ran away with the preacher from
the other, and a two-headed calf was born on
a farm across town. Residents of Siddel Marsh
turned their attention to these more recent
events, and Lauren Hamilton's suicide became
part of the town's history.

The house didn't sell for a long time. Finally
a young couple bought it, but they were gone
within a month's time.

The house went through a series of short-
term renters, but no one wanted to live there
for any length of time. It finally reverted to the
bank, who gave it to the local historical society.

The society made a valiant effort to restore it, but no one wanted to use it for teas or weddings or any of the other uses it might be put to.

At last even the historical society gave up. The windows were boarded and the doors were sealed, and the society told the town the house called Four Seasons was being "mothballed" for future generations. Since no one else wanted it either, there were no objections.

Over the years the house weathered. Some of the shutters gave way and fell into the grass or teetered precariously on the porch roof. The gardens became choked with weeds, although the plants in Lauren's knot garden proved hardy. They overgrew their boundaries and went to seed all along the shoreline. The wisteria continued to engulf the house until the back half of it sagged dangerously.

Children from Siddel Marsh dared each other to ride past the creepy old house, and a few hardy souls actually ran up onto the shaky porch and peered through the cracks. Those who did bolted away with eyes wide with fright and told of hearing sounds and seeing moving shadows deep within.

And on moonlit nights, music and laughter could be heard by anyone brave enough to venture close. A man's voice and that of a woman, it was said, but their words were indistinct.

After a while the house was avoided entirely.

SWEET FURY by Catherine Hart. She was exasperating, infuriating, unbelievably tantalizing, but if anyone could make a lady of the girl, it would be Marshal Travis Kincaid. And Travis swore that he'd coax her into his strong arms and unleash all her wild, sweet fury.

___2947-2 $4.50 US/$5.50 CAN

SILVERSWORD by Lindsay Randall. Shunned by the superstitious villagers and condemned by her own father, beautiful, headstrong Mara fled her home at the first opportunity. But the tempting embrace of a mysterious stranger created all but an impossible dream of love.

___2948-0 $3.95 US/$4.95 CAN

MISTRESS OF THE SUN KING by Sandra DuBay. Lovely Athenais de Montespan yearned for the love of the one man in all France who could fulfill her passion, handsome, sensual Louis XIV. But first she was forced to confront a rival for her lover's affections.

___2990-1 $3.95 US/$4.95 CAN

MADELINE BAKER

"LOVERS OF INDIAN ROMANCES HAVE A SPECIAL PLACE ON THEIR BOOKSHELVES FOR MADELINE BAKER!"   *—Romantic Times*

LACEY'S WAY
__2918-9 $4.50

RECKLESS LOVE
__2910-3 $4.50 US/$5.50 CAN

LOVE IN THE WIND
__2893-X $4.50 US/$5.50 CAN

RECKLESS HEART
__2915-4 $4.50 US/$5.50 CAN

FIRST LOVE, WILD LOVE
__2838-7 $4.50

RENEGADE HEART
__2744-5 $4.50

RECKLESS DESIRE
__2667-8 $4.50 US/$5.50 CAN

LOVE FOREVERMORE
__2577-9 $3.95 US/$4.95 CAN